| INITIAL HERE | DESCRIBE THIS BOOK IN ONE WORD... |
|---|---|
|  |  |
|  |  |
|  |  |
|  |  |
|  |  |
|  |  |
|  |  |
|  |  |
|  |  |
|  |  |
|  |  |
|  |  |
|  |  |
|  |  |

BRADLEY BEACH LIBRARY

If you're interested in writing a complete review, send us an email: sharlene@bradleybeachlibrary.org

For Enid

majestically. When Tom was alone up there, he felt close to the earth and sky and enjoyed a great sense of freedom as he overlooked the town.

Carbon County, Ridgeton, Pennsylvania, was the best anthracite coal-mining region in the United States, comprising less than five hundred square miles and including Lackawanna, Luzerne, Schuylkill, and Northumberland, and Carbon County itself. Coal had been mined there since the American Revolution, but coal mining did not become economically important until after the Industrial Revolution.

Every adult male in Ridgeton worked for Smedwick's Coal Mine, and any evening you would see their blackened faces as they straggled up Main Street in twos and threes, looking like Al Jolson singing "Mammy." Some were eighteen, having just graduated from Ridgeton High School, and some were only seventeen, having already dropped out. They spoke in low voices, complaining about the wages, the boss, the job itself. But no one thought of going elsewhere for a better job, because having a job—any job—in the Great Depression was an achievement in itself, even if they were stuck with a dead-end one. But they reserved the right to complain.

When Tom had graduated from Ridgeton High School the previous June, he did not go down the mine, preferring to stick with the job he had at Henze's Grocery Store. Since his junior year in high school, he'd worked after school at Henze's, and all day on Saturday, but now he was working full time. He would much rather work at the store than go down the mine, though it didn't pay that much. He dug in his heels as his father and his elder brother, Jim, kept pointing this out.

"I refuse to go to work down the mine!" Tom boldly announced to his mother yet again. Elizabeth Blaine backed her son, wanting him to become a high school teacher, just as she'd wished to become before dropping out of Teachers' Training College in Scranton for lack of funds. Tom had earned excellent grades in school, so he'd applied to Lehigh University in Bethlehem, Pennsylvania, hoping for a scholarship. But nothing had happened, so he'd stayed on with his job at Henze's Grocery Store—at least for the moment.

At eighteen, after graduating from high school, Jim had gone to work for the mine; now he was twenty-one. Their sister, Sarah, was nineteen and had won a scholarship to Scranton University, where she majored in French, planning to teach it in high school. Sarah's tuition grant paid only part of her expenses; she got the rest from summer jobs and from her father. Their kid brother, Luke, was fifteen and a freshman at Ridgeton High School, but he was considered too young to have an opinion in the family, or at least his siblings did not wish to hear it. The Blaine family was split down the middle, Jim and his father on one side and Tom, Sarah, and Mother on the other. Luke didn't count for much; nobody sought his opinion about anything.

Tom was fortunate to have his mother's support, because his father and elder brother were always picking on him. Out of deference to his wife, John used Jim as a cat's-paw to attack his middle son. But if John were provoked, he'd side with Jim, although Tom knew that his father's bark was worse than his bite. John Blaine had but one conviction: every young man in Ridgeton must go down the coal mine, and being a clerk in a grocery store was to have no job at all—at least not a job a man could be proud of. "How can you call it a job when you come home with your hands looking as lily white as when you left?" he chided his middle son.

Unless sorely pressed, Tom did not respond to these jibes. Jim was aware of his father's reticence with Tom. But that Sunday afternoon after dinner, Jim had sounded off, which pleased his father, who resented his wife's cosseting Tom as if she were still changing his diapers.

"Heck, Tom, why don't you let a girl have your job at Henze's?" Jim taunted.

Frowning, Tom ignored him.

"'Fraid to get your hands dirty?" Jim said, repeating his father's familiar jibe and taking advantage of his mother's being out of the kitchen.

"Cut it out, Jim!" John gruffly ordered.

"Dad, who does Tom think he is?" Jim protested.

"Haven't I told you that it's your mother's doin'?"

"Jim," Tom said, "why do you poke your nose in where it don't belong?" It stung to have to defend himself.

"So the worm turns!" Jim exclaimed.

"Don't call me a coward!" Tom protested, jumping up red-faced.

"What are you goin' to do 'bout it?" Jim rose as well.

"Will you two shut up and sit down!" John growled, afraid that Elizabeth would overhear the fracas. He got up and went to sit down in his wife's rocking chair by the stove to read the *Ridgeton News*.

"Dad, where do I stand?" Jim asked, seeing that his father had raised the newspaper to hide his face. "Ain't I kickin' in half my dough? All I wanna know is when Tom's goin' to do the same?"

"Jim, it's as I've told you before, if not a thousand times," John said. "His mother wants him to have an education to become a high school teacher, just like she wanted to become. She had to give it up for lack of money, just like Tom will 'less I pay for it or he gets a scholarship, like Sarah did. You see, I ain't got the dough, and you can't get an education 'less you pays the spondulicks. So that's the long an' the short of it. Besides, ain't I already helpin' to pay for Sarah, who wants to become a high school teacher too? Why she wants to learn French is beyond me, 'cause we ain't French. But that's what she's got her heart set on, so there ain't nothin' further to be said."

During his rambling discourse, John appeared to be irritated. He'd covered his face with the newspaper because his sons were destroying the peace of Sunday dinner.

"As far as I can see," Jim insisted, "Tom's already had more than enough education."

"How can anyone have too much education?" Tom protested, looking as if he were going to square off against his elder brother. That would have been unfortunate, for in fisticuffs, the solidly built Jim could quickly demolish his tall, skinny younger brother with one hand tied behind his back.

"Sit down, the two of you!" John growled, tossing aside the newspaper, determined to be reasonable for his wife's sake. "Jim, did I tell you what Principal Schenck told me 'bout Tom? I met him on Main Street the other day, and he told me how well Tom had done in high school. Those were his very words. So he said that it would be a shame if Tom didn't go to college. I told Principal Schenck that that was his mother's wish. But as yet it hasn't happened, and I can't pay for it."

"Dad, all I'm sayin' is that Tom has learned too much if you ask me," Jim said. "Now's the time for him to come to his senses and go down the mine like you and I did."

"Jim, I'm not goin' to work down the mine!" Tom angrily exclaimed. "And how can you say that I've had too much education?"

John's face flushed as he jumped to his feet, and he bellowed, "When you know so much that you're too proud to go down the mine! You spend all your time with your nose stuck in a book, fillin' your head with other people's ideas when you should be thinkin' for yourself about what you should do!"

"Oh, is that so?" Tom said, his face white from fear of his father.

"Oh, just like Miss Prim an' Proper," John said. "Did you hear that, Jim? Tom, whaddya take me for, a greenhorn? D'ya think you can pull the wool over my eyes?"

Silently Tom stood and listened to his father's complaints.

"Jim, this is all your mother's doin'. I ask you, Tom, who's feedin' you, an' clothin' you, and puttin' a roof over your head? I ask ya that!"

"Dad, I didn't say you weren't."

"All right, let's forget it! Parents are too damned soft these days, for they ask their kids, 'What is it that you want to do?' instead of tellin' 'em! An' if they don't happen to like what you suggest, you're supposed to go down on your hands and knees to 'em an' beg their forgiveness. I ask you, what's the world comin' to? When I was your age, my old man said, 'Come, m'boy.' And he took me down Smedwick's Coal Mine, where I worked at first as a coal sorter, for that's how I got started."

"Dad, don't think that I don't appreciate all that you've done for us," Tom said.

John turned to ask Jim. "Did ya hear that? Tom *appreciates* what I've done for him. Where does he get these la-de-dah words? Outta the dictionary, I suppose? Tom, speak to me in a language that I can understand instead of talking like Parson Stoppelmoor come to tea in the parlor."

While his father berated him, Tom stared at the slate floor of the kitchen with its band of sunlight. John insisted that his middle son stay with them after dinner and act like a member of the family. But Tom was sick and tired of his father always sounding off. He looked out the kitchen window at the green hill, yearning to be free to breathe the fresh air up there. From the summit he could look across the blue Appalachians and dream of his future. Stung by his father's words, he yearned to be free from family bondage—not that he didn't love his family, but he ached to lead a life of his own.

When they were little children, their father had read them the King James Bible every Sunday afternoon. He took more than two years to read the Old and the New Testaments; as he stumbled over difficult words, with Elizabeth correcting his pronunciation. Elizabeth and John had named their children after Bible figures: James and Thomas after Christ's disciples and Luke after the evangelist. Sarah was named for Abraham's wife, who'd borne Isaac in old age by divine intercession.

When Jim was born, John Blaine was making thirty-five dollars a week, and now that Jim had grown up and was working at the mine, he made as much money as his father. When the men came home on Friday evening, Elizabeth put her husband's pay packet in the sugar canister on the shelf above the stove and gave him two dollars a week spending money. Jim paid them half of his wages.

Now that the children had grown up, save for Luke, John was no longer reading the Bible for pleasure, but rather for the sake of argument, if you could call launching into Tom an argument. John had never been averse to the sound of his own voice, for he was dogmatic and hotheaded, a characteristic he'd bequeathed to Jim, while Tom had his mother's quiet, self-doubting nature. He was like Thomas in the Bible, having been a questioner all his young life.

John hoped that his middle son would grow out of his bookishness, which his mother thought a pity. For when he stopped learning and accepted his lot, he might just as well go down the mine. Elizabeth lived through the lives of her children and was determined that Tom should love learning. But she feared that failure might embitter him, making him pull his head in like a turtle into its shell. Her middle son's sense of superiority was no more than reserving the right to think for himself.

The two older men in the family were where the trouble arose; Tom would keep his opinions to himself until he crossed swords with his father or Jim, and an argument could quickly degenerate into physical violence. Two years before, after a Sunday dinner, an ill-considered remark of Tom's had so enraged his father that he'd

# CHAPTER 2

· · · · · · · · · · · · · · · · · · · · · · · · · · · · · · ·

TOM LEFT THE house through the opened kitchen door, heading up the alley between his house and that of Ray Dowling, the fire chief of Ridgeton. When Tom reached Main Street, he zipped up his leather jacket against the cool air, for it was late September and there was a light breeze. He hardly noticed the two-story, red brick houses lining either side of Main Street. The clock in the window of Preston's Mobil Station told that it was already after two o'clock. He wore his brown chinos and the sneakers he'd worn to play basketball in Ridgeton High School; he wore his good shoes only to church and Sunday school or for better occasions.

When Tom reached the foot of the hill, he began running like a mountain goat, leaping over outcropped boulders. His father's harsh words faded from his mind as his heart beat faster. When he'd reached the summit, he didn't even feel winded. He let out a shout to pierce the sky, which he felt he could almost reach out and touch. White cumulus clouds were sailing majestically above the earth.

At such moments, Tom felt alone with the earth and the sky, which was when he was happiest. There he could dream of the day when he'd prove himself to his family and the whole world. No longer would he be ridiculed, because he'd make some great discovery, like Pasteur, to benefit all of humankind. Or like Marconi, he'd transmit a radio signal around the world. Or like "Lucky Lindy," he'd fly solo across the Atlantic Ocean.

Tom sat down in the deep grass and looked up, bemused by his thoughts: *Do the clouds sail across the sky with a supreme indifference to man's fate? Would they look the same if no one was looking at them? If I could fly across the sky, I'd visit the distant corners of the earth. But the trouble is that my life's already been mapped out for me. I might just as well die or not bother living until I become old—if I get that far! Sleep, seven hours a night—call it oblivion. Get up in the morning and have orange juice, porridge, two fried eggs and bacon, and a slice of toast with butter and jam, and a glass of milk—call that breakfast, over and done with. Then I'll go to Henze's Grocery Store from seven to six. That's another day gone, to be scratched off on the calendar! God, how can I go on living like this forever when I wish to reach up and touch the sky?*

"Well, look who's up here!"

"Huh!" Tom exclaimed, quickly jumping up.

"You're not very welcoming—or very articulate for that matter, I must say!" Nola Henze's blue eyes sparkled in the sunlight and her blonde hair rippled lightly in the breeze.

"Nola, you startled me!" Tom said. "I didn't see you coming."

"I know you didn't," Nola replied, sitting on an outcropping rock as she raised her corduroy collar against the light breeze.

Tom stood and watched her cross her legs, which were also clad in brown corduroy.

"Why don't you sit down?" she asked.

"Nola, were you aware that I was—"

"You were what?"

"That I was up here?"

"What makes you think that?" Nola asked, smiling.

"Why did you come up here then?" Tom asked, frowning.

"Perhaps I wanted some fresh air? Besides, anyone can come up here if they wish to, can't they?"

"I didn't say they couldn't," Tom replied. "So, why'd you come up?"

"You've already asked me that question once." Nola laughed as she looked up at the cumulus clouds casting blue shadows over the Appalachians.

"Why don't you answer me?"

"Didn't I?" Nola asked, still looking the sky.

Tom sat back down in the deep grass and stretched out, closing his eyes. He could see the movement of the bright clouds casting a shadow over him as he wondered why Nola was sitting close beside him with her quick smile and playful, teasing manner. Had she come to surprise him?

He'd known Nola all his life, for they'd been in the same grades at school, attended Sunday school at the Lutheran Church, and graduated from the same class in high school. Tom didn't find it difficult to talk with Nola, so he didn't treat her differently just because she was a girl.

*What's Nola got in mind?* Tom asked himself. *Maybe it's more than just friendship.*

In high school Tom hadn't dated, not that he didn't like girls. He often dreamed about them, but his role had been teacher's helper. If a girl—or a boy, for that matter—was having difficulty with math, biology, physics, or chemistry, Tom was ready to help. If a girl needed help, it didn't so much matter to him that she was a girl, he was so busy explaining. So Tom had lots of "girlfriends."

Jim was the exact opposite. He held the world's record for real girlfriends. He'd bring a girl home for Sunday dinner just as if he were getting serious and about to become engaged and married. But nothing would come of it. A month or two later, he'd bring another girlfriend home for Sunday dinner to meet Mom and Dad, just because it was time he got serious.

Jim had told Tom that there was something wrong with him, because he'd had a string of girlfriends while Tom hadn't had one. But Tom thought that if you kissed a girl and fell in love with her, that meant you intended to get married and assume the responsibility of supporting her and providing for your children, just like Mom and Dad had done. When Tom had broached this idea with Jim, he had wisecracked, "Tom, that's fallin' outta the fryin' pan into the fire!"

During their junior year, Nola had gotten the idea of paying Tom back for his help in high school by telling him that her father was looking for a boy to work after school in the grocery store and all day on Saturday. So she put in a good word for him with her father, and that's how Tom got the job. Nola worked there as well when it was busy. Otherwise she worked on the books upstairs or did what her mother wanted. Grace Henze was an invalid, and she lived in the apartment above the grocery store.

Owning the store made the Henzes feel that they were a cut above the hoi polloi; at least it did Nola's mother. Fred Henze couldn't concern himself with social position and would be surprised to learn he had such a thing. For him, owning a store conferred no privileges, save the dubious one of working all the hours that God sends.

Nola took after her mother while her brother, Burt, was just like his father. Six years older than Nola, during high school he'd worked afternoons in the store and all day on Saturday, just as Nola did. After graduating from high school, he'd married his sweetheart, Lucy, and become a salesman for a farm equipment company in Wilkes-Barre. Lucy's father owned Grogh's Tavern on

Main Street, and Grace never forgave her son for marrying beneath himself, by which she meant beneath herself.

"I thought you'd gone!" Tom suddenly exclaimed, opening his eyes.

"It's you who were gone!" Nola exclaimed, laughing, her blue eyes sparkling in the sunlight. "I believed you'd forgotten all about me!"

"No, I didn't!"

"What were you thinking about, with your eyes closed?"

"I was just thinking."

"You must have been thinking about something?"

"No, nothing in particular."

"I must say, that's a real accomplishment!"

"Do you remember in high school that kids would tell me I'd swallowed the dictionary?" Tom asked with a rueful smile.

"You were always interested in reading and learning."

"While the other guys had all the fun!" Tom exclaimed as he pulled himself to his feet.

"Maybe you had more fun than you think, getting all those A's."

"So why didn't I get a scholarship? Do you think that learnin' a lot of facts makes you any wiser?"

"Filling your head with facts doesn't make you any wiser," Nola conceded. "But I was always grateful for your help, especially with chemistry."

"Well, I didn't have to know a lot of chemistry to help you," Tom confessed with a shrug of the shoulders.

"Thanks a lot!" Nola exclaimed.

"Nola, I didn't mean it that way!"

"How did you mean it?"

"I see that I've offended you."

"Not particularly, but then I didn't much like chemistry."

"My problem is that I don't accept the fact that I've no higher education."

"You never did accept that."

"Why do you think you know me better than I know myself?"

"I know you better than you think I do," Nola insisted, looking closely into his brown eyes.

"Tell me about myself."

"Well, there are two of you, Tom."

"Only two?"

"Yes, at least for the moment!"

"Do you really think so?"

"Yes, in fact, I really do!" Nola smiled.

"Well, tell me what they are?"

"The first is the mental Tom, who's way behind the physical," Nola said, hesitating.

"So, I'm just like everyone else?" Tom asked dismissively.

"Only with you, Tom, they're not on speaking terms."

"But Nola, I'm neither mental nor physical, not one or the other entirely," Tom insisted.

"Who said that you were?"

"Let's forget about me!"

"Is that your solution?"

"It is. You should try it!" Tom lay down in the deep grass and closed his eyes, asking himself if Nola had climbed the hill just to argue with him. He could feel his heart beating in his neck.

*Is Tom asleep?* Nola wondered. *Shall I speak to him?* "Tom?" *Now, he's pretending to be asleep!* She saw the muscle of his neck twitched. *Tom can be so maddening!* She reached out to touch his face, but she did not—not even to touch it ever so lightly.

For months Nola had thought about Tom, not knowing why. That Sunday afternoon she'd climbed the hill in hopes of finding him, deciding he wasn't like any other boy she'd ever known. Dave

Coulton would have made a pass at her by this time. He would have told her how much he loved her and that she was like a precious jewel that the Arab traders would refuse to sell at any price, or some such nonsense as that. But Tom didn't talk like that, because he was always too busy explaining himself.

*I'll bet he won't even hold my hand. Let's just be friends, he'd say. Let's crack the books together! That's the way it will always be with Tom. Let's just be friends.*

"Tom, are you asleep?"

"No, I was just thinking," he replied, opening his eyes and looking up at her.

"I should be getting home," Nola said, looking down over the rooftops of Ridgeton.

"Nola, do you mind if I walk you home?" Tom asked as he stood up.

"I don't mind at all—if you don't fall asleep!" Nola exclaimed, laughing.

"I wasn't sleepin'!" Tom insisted, grinning as he extended his hand to her.

Tom pulled her up so abruptly she fell against him with an "Oh!"

"I'm sorry!" he said, holding her slim body against him a moment longer than was necessary to restore her balance.

"Tom, if you don't wish to walk me home, you don't have to," Nola suggested when he'd released her.

"But, Nola, I want to," he insisted as they started down the path between the gray outcropping of boulders.

"What if I told you that I didn't want to see you?" Nola addressed his back as she was following him.

He turned with a look of surprise. "Why would you say that."

"Because it might be inconvenient for you," Nola said, a smile on her lips.

"Nola, don't you like being with me?" Tom asked, looking into her blue eyes.

"Why do you think only of yourself?"

"I'm not thinking of myself right now."

"Tom, do you really want to be with me?" she asked, meeting his brown eyes with hers.

"Yes, I like being with you a lot."

Nola jerked her head and laughed, her blonde hair shimmering in the sunlight.

When they'd reached the bottom of the hill, Tom wondered if he should have spoken his true feelings to her. *After all, why should Nola be interested in me? In Ridgeton the Henzes are regarded as moneyed people. They own the grocery store, while my father works at the mine. When Mr. Henze goes to work in the morning, all he has to do is go downstairs. Nola can go shopping in Wilkes-Barre or Philadelphia or even to New York to buy clothes. In Wilkes-Barre she can stay overnight with her brother and her sister-in-law. On Saturday night she always has a date for the double feature at the Alhambra and can choose any number of boys to accompany her, even though she's considered flighty because she's necked with a lot of them. She'd been going steady with Dave Coulton, and I've seen them necking in the balcony of the movie house.*

When Tom had gone to work at the grocery store, Nola had asked him what was bothering him, for he was always regarded as shy and a loner, but he'd always worked steadily and tried to please the customers. At lunchtime he'd take a paperback off the rack in the front of the store and sit on a milk crate in the backyard to eat the sandwich and drink the half pint of chocolate milk that her father had let him take from the fridge. When he'd finished lunch, he'd return the paperback to the rack, his reading to be resumed the next day—if he hadn't found another, having given up on the first.

Tom wasn't happy unless he had his nose in a book. Newspapers and magazines didn't much interest him, only books.

Like the other girls Tom had helped with homework, Nola thought, *He is, well, just Tom. Nobody is going to change him, least of all a girl.* Nobody really knew why Tom hadn't dated a girl, because he liked to talk with girls a lot. He was just different, but always himself. He never bragged as other boys did but was self-effacing in a humorous way.

Nola thought, *Actually he is very much interested in what you have to say, treating you as if you have a mind of your own. What mind?!*

But that was why Nola had broken up with Dave Coulton after they'd gone steady for almost a year. He'd delivered his ultimatum: "Nola, it's sleep with me or else." So Nola had dropped him. No guy was going to treat her like that—not even Tom Blaine!

By the time they'd reached Preston's Mobil Station, the silence between them was deafening.

Nola glanced at the lighted clock in the gas station window. *How could it already be six o'clock?*

Tom quickly followed her up the alley between the store and the Dinckmans' home next door to hers. In the backyard was the one-car wooden garage where Fred Henze housed his black Buick Straight-8.

"Tom, I'll be seeing you at work tomorrow," Nola said, turning around at the foot of the stairs leading up to the Henzes' apartment.

"Yeah," Tom replied, thrusting out his hand.

Surprised, Nola took his hand, wincing under the firmness of his grip. When he released her hand, she dashed up the stairs to the wooden porch above. She turned and called down, "Goodnight, Tom!"

"Goodnight, Nola!"

"Are you goin' home?"

"Yeah, I am!" Tom called back, turning and heading up the

alley between the buildings, his heart wildly beating as he heard Glenn Miller's "Tuxedo Junction" coming from the Dinckmans' front parlor. A few minutes later, he walked up the alley and saw the kitchen light in the window of his house. He knew his mother was waiting to serve him dinner.

# CHAPTER 3

· · · · · · · · · · · · · · · · · · · · · · · · · · · · · · · ·

"Tom, where've you been?" Elizabeth asked her middle son, laying aside her book and getting up from the rocking chair beside the stove.

"I know I'm late," Tom muttered, sitting down at his place at the table.

Elizabeth put a plate with two fried eggs and two sausages before him. "Be careful. It's hot!"

"Mom, it's gettin' colder outside," Tom said.

"I wouldn't know, not having been out!" Elizabeth said coolly.

"I guess you wouldn't," Tom said, staring at the eggs' crisp, seared edges and hard yolks.

Elizabeth took out her sewing box and sat down on the rocking chair to darn her husband's socks.

After cutting a piece of sausage, Tom put it into his mouth. "It's hot!" he exclaimed.

"Didn't I just say so?" Elizabeth scolded him, looking up.

"Yeah, I guess you did."

Tom wished to live on fresh fruits and vegetables and fish from the South Sea Islands. Maybe that's why he was as thin as a rail. But tonight he felt hungry and ate like a starving man. The undersides of the fried eggs were crunchy, looking glassy. When he'd finished eating, his mother poured him a cup of tea, then added milk and two teaspoons of sugar.

Tom knew that his mother was angry with him for coming home late and wanted an explanation. But he didn't like having to explain himself. *Besides,* he thought, *why doesn't she ever expect an explanation from Jim? Why does she treat him differently?*

Once when she had questioned Jim as to where he'd been, he'd said, "Out." So she didn't bother to ask him any more, and that was the end of it. With Tom it was different, though he didn't like to have her noticing him. Elizabeth had often told him that if he could come and go sight unseen, like a ghost, she'd be perfectly happy. But she wanted her middle son to feel that he could trust her, because she knew that it wasn't in his nature to do anything foolish. With Jim, it was just different; he was Jim. That's why he wisecracked, "Tom, you ain't never goin' to have any fun!"

The sun is at the center of the planets, just as Elizabeth Blaine was at the center of the family, its heart and soul. Tom was only too aware of that fact as he drank his hot, sweet tea while casting furtive glances at his mother. He didn't like it when she made him feel guilty, almost preferring his father's anger.

*She's given me birth. Does that mean she owns me?* Tom asked himself. *Why doesn't Mom treat Jim as if she owns him too? Is she always going to treat me like a child, eager to do her bidding?*

Recently Elizabeth had gone to Henze's Grocery Store, and Fred had wisecracked, "Mrs. Blaine, it seems that Tom's sweet on our Nola. But don't you worry about them, 'cause I don't expect anything to come of it."

That casual remark set Elizabeth's teeth on edge. *Why do the Henzes think they're somebody?* Elizabeth asked herself as she carried two bags of groceries along Main Street. *You don't see Grace anymore, although she always had her nose stuck in the air, just like her daughter, who runs her a close second, for she's cut from the same cloth. Now, if Fred Henze's wisecrack had been about Jim, I wouldn't have minded, because Jim's different. But Tom's inexperienced about girls, not understanding their feminine wiles. He hasn't spoken about Nola, and perhaps he won't ever. Maybe he's going to keep her a secret, just like Jim does with his girlfriends.*

"Tom, I don't want you upsetting your father like you did at dinner today," Elizabeth said, avoiding her real grievance. "You know that your father has your best interests at heart, even though, to be sure, he's a rough diamond. But he hasn't had your educational advantages."

"What educational advantages have I had?" Tom asked, creasing his brows. "I haven't had any more education than Jim and less than Sarah."

"But, Tom, you're the one who's always wanted an education. I know you're disappointed to not have received a scholarship."

"Don't worry, I'll get over it," Tom replied with grim irony.

"I suppose you will, but it would be a pity nonetheless," Elizabeth said with a sigh as she took up her darning.

"Where's Dad?" Tom asked, wishing to change the subject.

"Gone to Grogh's Tavern. Need you ask?" Elizabeth replied, a weary note in her voice.

"On Sunday night?"

"Lately your father's been going on Sunday nights as well, if you hadn't noticed."

"Dad figures that having taken you to church in the morning, he's done his good deed for the rest of the week?"

"Tom, that's uncalled for!"

"I'm sorry, Mom," he said. "So, where's Jim gone?"

"Who knows where Jim has gone, except out?" Elizabeth replied. "Meaning, don't ask."

"You always want to know where I've been, so why don't you ask Jim?"

"Because Jim's different from you, Tom," Elizabeth insisted for the umpteenth time.

"Where's Luke gone?"

"He's gone to Brian Murphy's to listen to Glenn Miller records. I expect him home shortly."

"Did Sarah go back to college?"

"No, but she'll be going to Scranton in the morning."

"So, where's she now?"

"She's gone to the dinner and dance at the Lutheran Church."

"Alone?"

"Of course not alone, with Dan Willoughby."

"With Dan Willoughby?"

"Yes."

"So, Sarah came home for the weekend, saying she wanted to see us, but goes with Dan to the dinner and dance," Tom said. "It seems to me that she must have known that Dan would be home from Lafayette College this weekend, so she really didn't come to see us, did she?"

"Tom, how can you be so naïve?" Elizabeth asked, laughing.

"So, if it weren't for the attraction of Dan, Sarah wouldn't even bother with us?" Tom asked.

"Whatever you say, Tom," Elizabeth replied, not wishing to discuss the matter.

"Mom, don't you worry about Sarah as much as you do about me?"

"How can you say such a thing, Tom, when you know how much I worry about all of you?"

"Well, please stop worrying about us," Tom insisted. "Besides, what could happen to us with you watching over us?"

"Tom, don't be so naïve."

"Mom, were you ever naïve?" Tom asked playfully. "If you ever were, I don't remember it."

"How far back does your memory go, Tom?" Elizabeth asked with a bland smile.

"Not too far, I guess!" Tom said, grinning.

Putting aside her darning, Elizabeth cut a slice of brown bread, which Tom buttered and smothered with strawberry jam. While he ate, she resumed her darning. The metal clock on the mantelpiece above the stove clicked metallically, emphasizing the silence. Beside it stood the sugar canister in which Elizabeth kept her housekeeping money.

"Goodnight, Mom!" Tom said as he got up from the table. "Maybe I'll read something before I go to sleep."

"Goodnight, Tom," Elizabeth replied, smiling.

Leaning over, Tom kissed the top of his mother's head where the brown hair was streaked with gray. Then he bounded up the narrow stairs to his small bedroom. His parents slept overlooking Main Street, while Jim and Luke shared the back bedroom. Sarah's bedroom was downstairs in the hallway between the kitchen and the front parlor.

Every hobby Tom had ever had was in evidence in his bedroom. The model airplanes of balsa wood and stretched doped paper propelled by rubber bands were hung by wires from the ceiling. On the bookshelf above the bed was his collection of American and foreign postage stamps with his pressed leaves beside it. In a shoebox above the bookshelf were his baseball cards, his favorite player being Ralph Kiner of the Pittsburgh Pirates.

His butterflies were pinned to a board on the wall. He'd caught them with a butterfly net he'd made with a bamboo pole and a coat hanger with some muslin his mother had supplied. He'd caught tiger swallowtails, red admirals, and monarchs, then preserved them in formaldehyde before pinning them to the bulletin board. He'd put his collection of rocks in boxes and stored them under the bed. His books were on the bookshelf and in more boxes. Tom had been given so many books he didn't wish to keep that he'd given them away.

Mrs. Doerlinger, the baker's wife, told him one day, "Tom, Carl likes a good book, so we have too many." Tom had gone around to the Doerlingers', and she'd given him a stack of Zane Grey paperbacks. Tom read *The Riders of the Purple Sage* but gave the rest away. Mrs. Doerlinger liked Earl Stanley Gardiner's mysteries and gave Tom a stack of them, which he gave away, not bothering to read them. From the Carnegie Public Library on Main Street, he borrowed Richard Halliburton's adventures, and in high school he'd read Shakespeare's *Julius Caesar* and *Macbeth*, along with Walter Scott's *Ivanhoe* and George Eliot's *Silas Marner*.

About twice a year, Elizabeth would make a big fuss, claiming that she couldn't clean Tom's room because it was so cluttered. So Tom would clean it himself, which was a major job. He'd lug the boxes of books and rocks out into the hall so that he had to turn sideways to pass. Then when he'd swept the room with a corncob broom, he'd push the chest of drawers and the bed to the other side so that he could sweep. When Jim and Luke saw what a mess he'd made, they knew there'd be hell to pay if they did the same. But Tom always got away with it.

He'd pushed his iron bed with its thin mattress against the inner wall. The wooden dresser with the varnish mostly peeled off he'd placed at the head of the bed. His writing desk faced the bed, with the only window in the room above it. It looked out at the Dowlings' house next door. A *Webster's Collegiate Dictionary* he'd set on the table, a graduation present from the Reverend Stoppelmoor, along with the Parker 51 pen and pencil set his parents had given him for the same occasion.

Tom pulled out the wooden chair at his desk and sat down. A cool draft came through the window and struck his face. Even on the coldest nights, Tom slept with the window open, as he hated to breathe hot, stuffy air and longed to be outdoors. He looked up the word *bilious* in the dictionary and wrote down its meaning in the small notebook he always carried with him. He stood up, stretched, and then sat on the bed, hunching over. He had his elbows on his knees and his fingers running through his long, brown hair, which his father nagged him about. But Tom refused to cut, saying, "I'm not a Heinie!"

*Why does everyone criticize me because I'm different?* Tom asked himself. *Like Mom, and especially Dad.* Even Principal Schenck had told his dad, "Mr. Blaine, Tom's not like the other boys. He must march to the sound of a different drummer!" Tom could hear his father's retort: "Leave him to me, Principal Schenck, and I'll knock some sense into his head. You see, I've got this 'cat' for that purpose, and I use it on all my boys."

Tom unlaced his sneakers and pulled them off. Then he peeled off his socks and stuffed them into the sneakers before setting them beneath the bed. He unbuckled his belt and slipped out of his chinos, which he folded and draped over the chair beside the writing table. He unbuttoned his shirt, took it off, and hung it over the chair too. After taking off his underwear, he took his pajamas from the bottom drawer of the dresser and pulled them on. He lifted the bedclothes and slipped into bed, where he stretched out on his back, clasping his hands behind his head.

He could hear the metallic clicking of the cicadas outside. There were fewer of them now, because it was late September. Soon they would be silent, and he'd hear the occasional vehicle on Main

Street. But the constant hum of the cicadas made the silence only deeper, like bats' wings pressed against his ears, muffling the sound.

Tom placed his hands on his thighs, for he could hear his heartbeat. *Does anyone ever ask himself why consciousness is such a burden? Could I find the answer to that question in a book? Why do you always say that you'll find the answer to any question in a book? Why don't you start thinking for yourself, like Dad says, instead of reading all the time? If you started thinking, even if only for a little bit, who knows where you might end up? You might even become a great inventor like Thomas Edison. Or a great industrialist like Andrew Carnegie. Or a great financier like J. P. Morgan. So what's stopping you? Isn't it only your self-doubts and fears?*

Tom chastised himself. *Your problem is that you've got to stop thinking about yourself!*

*I've seen Nola a thousand times, yet I can't remember what her face looks like. If I fall asleep and dream, will I see what her face looks like? And is her face always the same, or is it different at different times? If I touched her would she feel as soft as she looks? If I held her naked body in my arms—but I wouldn't do that, not unless we were married! Am I in love with Nola Henze? And if I am, does that mean I've forgotten myself?*

"I gotta get some sleep!" Tom muttered, dispelling such futile thoughts. He turned onto his stomach and pressed his face into the pillow. Immediately he felt that he was falling into a spiral down a vortex.

*Is sleep nothing more than waiting to regain consciousness?* Tom asked himself. *Do you wake up the same person you were when you fell asleep or someone different?*

"Tom?"

Startled, he sprang from the bed and opened the door, saying, "Sarah, whaddya want?"

"Tom, I've got great news for you!" Sarah exclaimed as she put her arms around him, pressing her cheek against his.

"What great news?" he asked, switching on the light.

"Dan's father's goin' to speak with the admissions director at Lafayette College," she said breathlessly.

"What for?"

"Because Dan's father's a trustee at Lafayette, and he's going to find out why you haven't heard."

"Sarah, they don't have to give you a reason."

John asked from the foot of the stairs, "Sarah, have you finally come home?"

"Tom, I know you'll get a scholarship!" Sarah called down the stairs, taking the deed for the word.

"Heavens be praised!" Elizabeth exclaimed. She had been awakened by the commotion and had come to the foot of the stairs too.

"Sarah, I haven't got a scholarship!" Tom cried.

"But, Tom, you will!" she insisted.

John turned and asked Elizabeth, "Lafayette College ain't lookin' for me to pay?"

"Shut up, John—and be proud of your son!" she said.

# CHAPTER 4

• • • • • • • • • • • • • • • • • • • • • • • • • • • • • • • • • • •

AT SIX-THIRTY IN the morning, Tom got up and dressed quickly. In the kitchen his mother was preparing breakfast. His father and Jim had already left for Smedwick's Coal Mine, while Sarah and Luke were still asleep.

"Sarah! Luke!" Elizabeth called.

"Good morning, Mom!" Tom said, taking his place at the table.

"Mornin' to yourself!" Elizabeth said, ladling the porridge into the bowl before him.

Tom put cream and sugar on his porridge, which tasted as if it had been cooked too long, while his mother scrambled him two eggs and fried two links of sausage.

When he had finished eating his eggs and sausage, Elizabeth cut him a thick slice of brown bread, which he buttered and covered with a heaping spoonful of strawberry jam.

"Sarah! Luke!" she called again.

"Coming, Mother!" Sarah called back.

"Sarah, pull the covers off Luke," Elizabeth ordered.

"Luke, get up!" Sarah called.

Having finished his cup of tea with milk and two spoonfuls of sugar, Tom was well aware that his mother had hardly spoken to him. She wanted an explanation as to why he'd come home late the night before.

But instead of explaining, he called, "See you, Mom!" as he dashed upstairs.

"Tom, where you goin'?" Sarah asked, for he had almost collided with her. "Mother, why is Tom always in such a hurry!"

"Sarah, did you wake up Luke?" Elizabeth asked, ignoring her question.

"Luke, will you get up?!" Sarah called upstairs.

"Okay, I'm gettin' up," Luke groaned.

"Now!" Sarah called again.

While putting on his leather jacket, Tom dashed downstairs and called, "See you later, Mom!" Then he left the house through the open kitchen door.

"Good-bye, Tom!" Elizabeth called after him, thinking that he'd make something of himself if he could only figure out how. *Maybe Tom* will *get a scholarship and go to Lafayette College,* she thought. *Maybe he'll major in agriculture and become the county agricultural agent. Maybe he'll take up animal husbandry so that he can tell the dairy farmers why their cows have ceased to give milk or whatever it is that ails them. I know Tom's going to better himself more than anyone ever expects, even himself.*

As Tom approached the grocery store, he saw Principal Schenck swing his Chrysler Imperial into Preston's Mobil Station and stop before the gas pumps.

"Hiya!" Tom called to him.

"Howdy do, Tom!" Principal Schenck called as he stepped

out of the car and waved his hand. "Tom, did you ever hear from Lafayette College?"

"Not a word, Principal Schenck."

"That so?" Schenck frowned as he stepped into the gas station office.

"Principal Schenck, did Bud speak to you yet?" Ike Preston asked, looking up from his desk, where he was busy doing paperwork.

"Bud's under the bay, servicin' a car," Schenck replied.

"You want it filled up?"

"Yeah, fill it up."

"Lemme think. Bud found these letters. If I could just lay my hands on 'em," Ike said. Then he called out to Bud, who was filling the principal's tank, "Where'd you put those letters for Principal Schenck?"

"Cathy McKeon's letters?" Bud called.

"What letters?" Schenck asked, his brow knit.

"Gas an' electric an' phone bill. They're around here somewhere, Principal Schenck," Ike said. "Bud, where'd you put those letters?"

"Ike, I gave 'em to you," Bud said, having filled Schenck's car.

"Bud, did you see where I put 'em?

"You put 'em beneath the counter."

"So I did!" Ike exclaimed, plucking out the letters, which he handed to Schenck. "All stamped and ready for delivery at the post office!"

"Thanks, Ike," the principal replied tersely, smiling grimly as he thrust the letters into his raincoat.

At Ridgeton High School, Schenck went straight to Cathy McKeon's office and dropped the letters smack dab in the middle of her desk. "Where did you find these letters?" she asked, seeing that the first was addressed to the director of admissions at Lafayette College.

"They were under the driver's seat of your car, Cathy," Schenck said, looking aggrieved.

"Principal Schenck, why were you looking beneath the driver's seat of my car?" Cathy asked, sounding aggrieved.

"Ike Preston just handed them to me," Principal Schenck said, hardly able to control himself. "Bud found 'em while he was servicin' your car."

"How could that be, when I'd mailed them?" Cathy asked.

"Cathy, you didn't mail them any more than you paid the electric and gas bill!" Schenck stomped into his office, which was connected to his secretary's.

Cathy went to the door of his office and asked, "Will you tell Tom Blaine that his letter wasn't sent?"

"Of course I will!" Schenck thundered, and he slammed the door shut.

❈ ❈ ❈

When Tom entered Henze's Grocery Store, Fred called to him from the storeroom at the back, "Tom, is that you?"

"Yeah, it is, Mr. Henze!"

"Ready to start work, are you?"

"You kiddin', Mr. Henze?" Tom replied, taking his apron from the hook at the back of the store opposite the storeroom.

"I thought maybe you'd won the lottery and didn't need to work anymore," Fred remarked as he straightened up and turned around.

"Sorry, I was five minutes late this morning."

"Forget it, Tom."

"Whatcha lookin' for, Mr. Henze?"

"A case of borscht. It's around here somewheres." Fred shuffled some cartons. "Mrs. Gottlieb was in yesterday and asked for some borscht, but I didn't have any on the shelf. A week ago I thought I'd ordered some, but maybe I didn't."

"Is that the red stuff that comes in a bottle?"

"Yeah, that's it—it's red and comes in a bottle," Fred said absently.

"What is it anyway, Mr. Henze?"

"What is what, Tom?"

"What's *bosh*?"

"It's *borscht*, and it's beet soup."

"I didn't know people drank beet soup."

"Well, the Jews do," Fred replied, still searching around. "The Jews eat it hot in the winter and cold with sour cream in summer."

"They put sour cream in their soup?"

"Yeah, ask Mrs. Gottlieb next time she comes in. She's about the only customer I've got for it, and she'll kick up blue murder if I don't have it in the store, like she did yesterday. I thought I'd ordered another carton, but maybe I didn't. I'll ask Nola if she'll ordered some, if she hasn't done it already."

"What's it taste like?"

"What's what taste like?"

"This beet soup."

"Whaddya think it tastes like?"

"Beets?"

"You've got it!" Fred said. "Tom, will ya sweep the floor, but before you do that, bring in the milk crates and bread cartons. I've already brought in the newspapers."

"Sure, Mr. Henze!" Tom replied brightly.

"Oh, Tom, there's another thing," Fred said. But Tom was already out the front door on his way to move crates of milk from Hoffman's Dairy and cartons of bread from Doerlingers' Bakery into the store. When he had finished that, he swept the floor with a corncob broom, including behind the counter.

All the while Tom was thinking, *Nola won't ever have to worry about money. As soon as she graduates from college, she'll marry some guy who's already got a good job lined up. Probably won't even bother to make him breakfast 'cause she'll have her own housemaid to do that. When she finally gets up, it'll probably be midmorning, and she'll have a coffee klatch with the lady next door. Nola's going to have a very pleasant, comfortable life, but maybe it will be a bit dull and uneventful. She'll listen to "Vic and Sade" on the radio every morning, wondering if Vic will get transferred to Peoria.*

*I'm sure she'll have a couple kids, and love them more than she loves her husband, who'll probably be too busy being a big shot even to notice. She'll probably join the Rolling Hills Country Club to take golf lessons, and she'll go to those afternoon tea parties at the country club where the ladies eat those small sandwiches with the crusts cut off. I wonder if Nola will be smug and self-satisfied, thinking that she's somebody, just because she's got a lot of money. But why shouldn't she? Still, I wonder if she will ever really be happy.*

"Mornin's are gettin' a bit nippy nowadays, Tom," Fred said, breaking into Tom's reverie as he was emerging from the storeroom, carrying a carton of borscht.

"You find the bosh, Mr. Henze?" Tom asked, looking up from sweeping the dust into the dustpan.

"Yeah, this is it, but it's pronounced *borscht,*" Fred said. "*Bosh* is what they called the Germans during the war when they didn't call 'em Krauts or Huns. Oh, Tom, I almost forgot. I want to have a word with you when you're havin' lunch. Nothin' very important, mind you. Just a friendly chat."

"Yeah, sure, Mr. Henze."

"Tom, haven't I asked you to call me Fred?"

"Sorry, Mr.—er—Fred."

Fred returned to the storeroom to look for something else, while Tom asked himself, *I wonder what Mr. Henze wants to talk to me about. Maybe my job's kaput. Anyway, it isn't much of a job. If I get fired, Dad and Jim will be pleased. They always say my job's too cushy, isn't a real job at all. Or maybe Fred Henze, wanting to get away from his nagging wife, slipped out to Grogh's Tavern last night and had a word with Dad. Maybe he and Dad were deciding my fate over a couple of beers. "Tom thinks that he can make a career outta bein' a clerk in a grocery store." That's what Dad would have said last night at Grogh's, or maybe Mr. Henze said that to Dad. Or maybe they both put their heads together and decided that they know me better than I know myself.*

All morning Tom's mind was filled with painful, useless self-interrogation. He began making small mistakes, getting down Kellogg's Wheaties when the lady wanted Kellogg's Cornflakes, or he began giving the wrong change. He was sick with apprehension when Nola came downstairs at eleven o'clock and greeted him offhandedly. Or so he thought, for she'd said "Hi!" with a funny half smile, which seemed to say that she knew something he didn't. Quickly she'd disappeared, going upstairs saying she had the books to do.

*It's Monday morning. So why does Nola have the books to do? Wouldn't she have finished doing the books on Saturday? Maybe she just wants to double-check her work, even though she probably already double-checked it on Saturday. Why did she give me a funny smile? And why did she act as if she knows something I don't? I'll bet her smile's got something to do with her father's friendly chat with me at lunchtime. Maybe Fred—more likely her mother—is thinking I'm getting too serious with her. But what have I said to her?*

*Tom, stop makin' a big deal outta nothin'! Don't act like a jerk! As Jim says, you're like a weak sister! For crissake, not even Luke would go on like this! Jim would face up to the situation, whatever it might be. But I'm not Jim, I'm different.*

At five minutes to noon, Tom left the cash register and went back to the storeroom, where Fred was again shuffling cartons, looking for something.

"Mr. Henze, can I go home for a minute?" Tom asked him.

"Yeah, sure, Tom," Fred replied, straightening up and turning around. "That little chat of ours can wait."

"Oh, I forgot about that!"

"Tom, please call me Fred."

"Yeah, sure—er—Fred!"

The red brick houses on Main Street looked begrimed in the noonday sun, but Tom hadn't noticed them.

*You aren't the only one who's got to worry about the future,* Tom told himself, loping along, his arms cleaving the air. *Compared to the other guys who graduated from high school with you, you're lucky. Unlike them, you didn't have to go to work down the mine. So you should be grateful.*

Suddenly he changed his mind and stopped, then began retracing his steps back to Henze's Grocery Store. He felt a tightness in his chest; he was hardly able to breathe, as if he were being suffocated or was about to be sick.

*You're a coward! You've no guts! You've built this whole friggin' thing up outta nothin'!*

Tom stopped again and looked around at the houses along Main Street as if he were seeing them for the first time. There wasn't a person in sight, and the street looked strangely empty.

*The kids are at school, or maybe they're home having lunch.*

He walked up the narrow alley between the store and the Dinckmans' house. Some empty wooden crates stenciled with "Hoffman's Dairy" were stacked behind the store. The backyard, enclosed by a chain-link fence, was lined with clumps of ragweed. At the back was the one-car, wooden garage with Fred's black Straight-8. Rank-smelling ailanthus overarched the fence, and Tom could see their pinnate leaves, which in spring would bloom with inconspicuous, yellow-green flowers.

Tom upended a crate and sat down as he'd done every day, except in winter, when he ate lunch in the storeroom. *Fred's probably upstairs now, having lunch with Grace—or more likely he's fixin' her lunch and listenin' to what she's got to say about me. I don't feel much like lunch myself. Ugh!* Tom quickly grabbed a milk crate and threw up into it, even though there was hardly anything in his stomach. As he straightened up, his stomach felt as if it were full of hot peppers. He hid the milk crate in the ragweed.

"Tom, are you out there?" Fred called through the screen door.

"Yeah, Mr.—er—Fred!"

"Had your lunch, as yet?"

"Nope."

"D'ya wan' me to bring you a sandwich?"

"I was just comin' for one myself."

"Stay right where you are, and I'll bring you something," Fred replied. "Doncha like a bologna sandwich and a chocolate milk?"

"Yeah, that's right!"

When Fred's figure disappeared from behind the screen door, Tom sprang to the spigot protruding from the foundation of the store, where he cupped his hands and slurped up some water, which he spat out to clear the taste of vomit from his mouth.

Fred reappeared a few moments later, carrying a cellophane-wrapped sandwich in one hand and a half-pint carton of chocolate milk in the other, while Tom was already seated on an upturned wooden crate.

"Tom, is everything okay at home?" Fred asked, handing him the sandwich and milk.

"Thanks, yeah, sure is, Mr.—er—Fred," Tom quickly replied.

"Now, about this little chat we're goin' to have." Fred grabbed a milk crate and sat down beside him. "I know you haven't missed a day's work since you started, not anyways that I can remember. So, you've been very conscientious. If you wanna stay right here and learn the grocery business, I'll teach ya the ropes. Maybe I can even pay you a bit more, but not too much more—not at first anyway. You're a bright and go-ahead boy, but maybe you don't wanna learn the grocery business. Maybe you've got big ideas of your own and don't wanna stay in a dull place like Ridgeton. You see, when I started out I didn't have anything, but I was smart enough to marry the boss's daughter, a gal who had somethin'. So you see, Tom, I don't believe in denyin' a young fella his chances, 'specially if he's got ambition. I expect if you'd asked your father if he wanted to go down the coal mine when he was your age, he'd tell you that he didn't have a choice. So, Tom, it's your decision to make if this is the opportunity that you're seeking. Do I speak too plainly?"

"No, not at all, Mr.—Fred!" Tom responded, thinking that the offer was contingent on his marrying Nola. *That's the way to have a steady job for life!*

"Well, Tom, think it over," Fred said, placing his hands on his knees. "Oh, another thing: Burt's got no interest in the store. So my son won't be standin' in your way. Besides, I don't expect to be around forever. And who knows, I might even decide to retire and go to Florida and live off the guv'mint. Well, Tom, think about it and take all the time you want."

"Thank you, Fred. I will," Tom exclaimed, jumping up when Fred did, with a bright smile on his face.

When Fred went into the store, Tom choked down his bologna sandwich, then swilled down the chocolate milk, saying to himself, *Fred, I accept your offer! That's what I should have said right from the start when he asked me and be done with it. What better offer do I expect to have anyway? I didn't get a scholarship, and Dad can't afford to pay for me. Besides, if Dad had his way, I'd have been working at Smedwick's Coal Mine since last June. Maybe if Fred pays full time, he'll pay for me to go to college too, and I won't have to pay him back, because I'll be married to Nola.*

*Maybe Nola will want kids right away, and I won't be able to afford it without working in the grocery store. Maybe Fred has already spoken to Nola about the offer he was going to make me. Is that why she looked so funny this morning? Between the two of them, they've got the wedding date set, and for crissake I haven't yet found the courage to kiss her!*

Sitting down on the milk crate, Tom hunched over, his elbows on his knees and his head below his shoulders.

*If I did what Dad wants, I'd work forty years down Smedwick's Coal Mine—more than two times my present age! But maybe I wouldn't live that long, but get killed in a mine explosion or maybe be gassed. But if I didn't die before I was sixty-five, I could retire and start living on my pension or Social Security. But maybe I wouldn't have that many years to look forward to. Maybe I'd just sit in the backyard and feel the sun's warmth on my face, the sun I hadn't seen for so many years because I'd been burrowing down in the earth like a mole. I'd probably be suffering from emphysema or black lung disease too. I wouldn't be able to draw a deep breath, but what would I need breath for except to tell myself how stupid I'd been to work all those years down the mine for peanuts? After all those years or maybe only a few, I'd have become inured to work. So by then it probably wouldn't matter, because my spirit would be broken.*

Suddenly Tom straightened up and asked himself, *What's the use of speculating about something so remote? Who wants to be thirty anyway? When you're thirty, you're already middle-aged, so even if you don't know it, your life's a sham. By that time, you won't be able to fight your way out of a paper bag, so it won't matter, 'cause it's too late for you, 'cause you don't have any future. You're just living from day to day, taking all the punches that life dishes out.*

*Maybe that's why everybody, including my dad ,says that I've built a wall around myself, withdrawing like a turtle into its shell, because I can't face up to life. Maybe I should go back to the womb—if only I could—and stop feeling so miserable about myself. Fred said he could wait: "Take all the time you want, Tom." But why should Fred Henze wait? No man wants to wait for an answer, because no man likes indecision, especially when he's making a serious business offer.*

Springing from the milk crate, Tom stepped past the screen door into the store. Fred was in the storeroom shuffling boxes again.

"Mr. Henze, I accept your offer!" Tom exclaimed, a bright smile on his face.

"Oh good, Tom," Fred replied absently, moving cartons around. Then he finally turned toward Tom. "I can give you twenty-two bucks a week, two more than you're now gettin'. If that ain't enough, I can understand a young fellow who's got irons in the fire."

"Sure thing, Mr. Henze!"

"Oh, Tom, will ya start callin' me Fred?"

"Sure will! Thank you—er—Fred!"

# CHAPTER 5

AT SIX O'CLOCK that evening, Elizabeth was in the kitchen, shelling lima beans. During his childhood Tom had helped her, doing even more than Sarah, who was always busy with extracurricular activities at high school. Once a week on Friday afternoons, Tom would scrub the kitchen floor and clean the bathroom. Often when he got home from school, Elizabeth would tell him about the book she'd been reading.

She had gotten Tom reading in the first place, for she always took books out of the library for him. When he was fourteen, he came home from school to find a biography of Oliver Cromwell on the kitchen table. He started reading it, and when Elizabeth arrived home from a PTA meeting at the school, she told him that he was reading her book. That was the beginning of Tom's adult reading, for after that he had no interest in boyish adventures.

"Fred Henze has offered to teach me the grocery business,"

Tom said to his mother. "He even suggested that I might someday manage the store."

"Manage it? Tom, you'll own it!" Elizabeth said. "Just you wait, Tom! I don't want to hear any more talk of sending you down Smedwick's Coal Mine! I won't hear of it! Tom, I can see the need of another store at the far end of Main Street, which would be more convenient for the people over there. You might put Jim in to manage it, and if he's not interested, you might consider Luke. By then it won't be called Henze's Grocery Store, but will be Blaine's, which would be more appropriate, seeing that you're to be the owner!"

Already Elizabeth saw her family usurping the Henzes' place among the commercial gentry of Ridgeton. She thought Tom might even outshine old Mr. Smedwick himself. Then she would go to the Lutheran Church on Sunday morning with a certain air of distinction.

"Mom, can I have supper early tonight?" Tom asked, interrupting her reverie.

"Have you somewhere to go?" she quickly asked.

"Nowhere in particular, just out."

"Out? Tom, you are beginning to sound like Jim!"

With a hapless grin, Tom dashed upstairs to wash up for supper. A few minutes later, when he'd reappeared in the kitchen, his mother took a meatloaf from the oven and cut him two thick slices, over which she'd ladled bubbling tomato sauce. Then she spooned a helping of mashed potatoes with peas beside them.

*Tom's a strange boy,* Elizabeth said to herself, casting a furtive glance at him while he ate. *Why doesn't he know his own best interest? He'll never succeed in life if he isn't prepared. Call it being practical! But being practical wasn't the Lord's gift to Tom, who'll always need his mother's advice. But I won't allow anyone to poke fun at him, saying, "Didn't I tell you so, Elizabeth?" No, not at my Tom, for he's different!*

Having finished his rice pudding and drunk his tea, Tom ran upstairs to put on his sneakers and grab his leather jacket. Leaving the house past the kitchen door, he quickly called good-bye to his mother and then ran up the alley into Main Street. He began to run like the wind, not stopping till he'd reached the summit of the hill, where he fell breathless into a hollow between two outcropping boulders. This was his favorite spot, and often he'd lain there dreaming his dreams of youth and of the future, feeling exhilarated.

*Why do I feel so happy?* Tom asked himself. *The road is stretching before me with all its twists and turns, and I feel so full of joy when I should feel miserable! Shouldn't I have left such thoughts behind? Haven't I plugged away long enough, feeling miserable and lonely, being alienated from my family—except for my mother and sister?*

Standing up, Tom saw the sun setting behind the Appalachians in the west, while the great dome of sky above was still light, with darkness slowly enveloping the earth. At that moment the earth seemed alive, a woman stirring in her sleep, her breasts the mountains and her thighs the dark valleys between.

*I will lie down beside her in the depths of night,* Tom thought. *Be the sun to her, and she will be my earth.*

Tom sat down in the deep grass, gazing at the fading sunlight in the west.

*What does her face look like?* he asked himself, turning onto his stomach and thrusting his hands deep into the grass, clutching it. *Why am I so inhibited? Does anyone care if I exist? Once I went to Philadelphia with the class from school and saw the Liberty Bell and Betsy Ross's house. Nola's been to New York City shopping, but the same sun shines in New York City that shines in Ridgeton, Pennsylvania, just like it shines in London, Paris, and Rome, and even the remotest places of the earth.*

Sitting up, Tom pressed the heels of his hands toward his eye sockets.

*What color are her eyes? In the sunlight are they blue with a shade that sometimes looks green?*

He looked up into the darkening sky. *That's Sirius, the Dog Star, the brightest star in the winter sky. I have to make something of myself and face up to life, even if Dad or Jim didn't. Mom wants me to become a teacher, while she couldn't. So neither of my parents got what they wanted, but if they had, they might not have married. Then none of us would have been born.*

Suddenly the moon rose above the mountains in the east, casting its silver radiance on the earth.

*Her eyes are beautiful and sparkle in the sunshine, and her golden hair ripples with the slightest breeze.*

"Tom, are you up here somewhere?"

*Her voice! I should run away!* Tom jumped up and took off, running wildly down the hillside, only to trip over an outcropped rock and to be sent careening into another, which struck his shoulder. A sudden, sharp jab of pain shot from his arm to his neck.

"Christ!" Tom groaned, clutching his right arm tightly as he lay on his side, writhing in the grass.

"Tom, where are you?"

"Here!"

"What happened?" Nola asked, kneeling beside him, touching his hair and his face.

"I tripped and hurt my arm."

"Do you think it's broken?"

"No, I don't think so. Nola, will you say something to me?"

"Like what?"

"Just say something."

"Tom, don't be silly, and get up."

"What time is it?"

"About nine o'clock."

Turning onto his back, clutching his arm, he gazed up into the dark heavens. "That's Orion up there," he said. "The bright stars are the shoulders and hips, while the faint ones that are aslant are the belt. That dull middle star in the belt isn't really a star at all; it's the nebula in the constellation of Orion."

"Tom, please get up!"

Tom sat up and hunched over, clutching his right arm. "Nola, may I walk you home tonight?" he asked, looking into her eyes in the silvery moonlight.

"If you wish, but now you must get up!"

"Nola, I'm almost a member of the family."

"I'll bet you think you are!" Nola exclaimed, laughing.

"'Don't be such an idiot, Tom.' Is that what you think?" he asked. "Don't be angry with me."

"I'm sorry if I disappoint you," Nola replied. "Can I help you to stand up?"

"No, thanks, I'll manage," Tom insisted, pulling himself to his feet, still clutching his right arm.

"How does your arm feel now?"

"It's okay."

"Let's go down by the path."

"But I wanna walk straight down."

"That's too dangerous in the dark. Haven't you hurt yourself already?"

"I guess my arm's feeling okay."

"It'll feel much better if you don't fall down again."

"How can I fall when I've got you to catch me?" Tom asked, putting his arm around her shoulders.

"Please keep to the path!"

"Do you think I'm stupid?"

"Sometimes I think you must be!"

"You think I'm stupid?"

"Yes, sometimes, but keep to the path!"

"How can I walk straight when you think I'm stupid?"

"I didn't say you were *always* stupid," Nola insisted. "I just said that sometimes you act that way."

"Nola, would you be happy if I blew my brains out?"

"Tom, you're not going to blow your brains out." Nola was unmoved by his protest. "Now we're coming to the bend."

"Nola, how can I impress you?"

"Why not try by being yourself?"

"You sound just like my mother!" he exclaimed with a rueful laugh.

"I'm not your mother! Please keep to the path."

"Nola, did you ever think that life can be ended in a split second?"

"Please don't wobble!"

"Doesn't that thought impress you?"

"Not particularly."

"Is that because it never occurred to you?"

"Of course it's occurred to me! I just don't think about it."

"Nola, I think you're very good for me."

"Why's that?"

"Because you keep me to the straight and narrow."

"Do you mean the path?"

"I mean what lies beyond."

"Beyond what?"

"Beyond the straight and narrow!"

"Tom, are you awake or just daydreaming?"

"Nola, sometimes I think that I haven't been awake for a single moment in my life."

"Why do you wake up now then?"

"Because, Nola, nothing in the world means so much to me as you do," Tom said, stopping and turning to her.

"Tom, are you quite sure about that?" Nola asked, looking closely at his face in the moonlight.

"I feel very sure about it, Nola, but really you don't know me."

"I know you well enough," Nola replied. "You're too self-conscious for your own good."

"Isn't it good to be self-conscious?"

"That all depends."

"On what?"

"On what it leads to."

"Do you think your father will fire me?" Tom asked.

"Why should he do that?"

"Maybe I should beat him to the punch and tell him that I quit his lousy job!"

"My father's very pleased with you, Tom," Nola insisted. "Why do you make such a fuss about it?"

"Nola, when I just told you that I love you, you didn't respond."

"Tom, you didn't tell me that you loved me."

"Yes, I just did."

"Tom, you're the livin' end!" Nola exclaimed with a light laugh.

"What did I just say then?"

"You told me that I meant more to you than anybody in the world."

"Isn't that the same thing?"

"No, it isn't!" she exclaimed.

"Is that why you didn't tell me that you loved me?"

"Perhaps."

"Perhaps what?"

"Perhaps I haven't made up my mind."

"When we get back to the store, may I kiss you goodnight?"

"Not if you're acting silly."

"When did I ever act silly?"

"Do you really wish to kiss me?"

"Yes, I do, but last night you ran upstairs."

"Tom, would other boys act like this?"

"Have I said anything to offend you?"

"No, Tom, you've never said anything to offend me. I've always enjoyed talking with you, even though I've usually had to do the listening."

"Didn't I hurt your feelings when I said that your father could keep his job?"

"No, you didn't."

"Why not?"

"Because I always expect you to speak your mind."

"Why doesn't that offend you?"

"Well, it doesn't because I've never known a boy like you who spoke his mind."

They walked in silence down the hillside. When they reached the bottom, Tom slipped his arm around Nola's waist as they walked along Main Street to the alley between Henze's Grocery Store and the Dinckmans'.

"Nola, I'll say goodnight," Tom sputtered when they'd reached the foot of the stairs.

"Goodnight, Tom," Nola replied. "Does your arm still hurt?"

"No, it's all right. Nola, I'd like to see your face in the moonlight."

"Why do you want to see my face?"

"I want to see what it looks like."

"Are you being serious?"

"Really, I can't remember what your face looks like."

"Maybe that's a good thing!" Nola exclaimed with a laugh.

"Your face is a mystery to me."

"I've never known a boy to say such a thing!"

"Nola, do you think that I can make you happy?"

"Will you have a doctor look at your arm?"

"My arm's all right."

"You don't want a doctor to look at it?"

"I will, I'm sure."

"Meaning you won't?"

"Nola, may I kiss you goodnight?"

"No!" Nola exclaimed, quickly turning around and dashing upstairs. But when she'd reached the top, she grasped the rail and leaned over, calling, "Goodnight, Tom!"

"Goodnight, Nola!" Tom called back as he headed up the narrow alley, his heart beating wildly.

On Main Street, the hill loomed darker before him, with the moonlight behind it. He walked up the alley between his house and the Dowlings, where he saw the kitchen light shining, knowing that his mother would be reading in her rocker, unable to sleep until her middle son was safely home.

# CHAPTER 6

∙∙∙∙∙∙∙∙∙∙∙∙∙∙∙∙∙∙∙∙∙∙∙∙∙∙∙∙∙∙∙∙∙∙∙∙∙

"Father, last night Tom came home with his arm black and blue," Elizabeth reported to John at five the following morning when he and Jim were having breakfast.

"What the blazes has the boy done now?" he muttered.

"Mom, was he drunk?" Jim asked with a smirk.

"All he'll tell me is that he fell, but he won't say any more," Elizabeth said, ignoring Jim's jibe.

"If a son of mine comes home drunk and sneaks into the house like a thief, then you needn't waste your breath tellin' me about it 'cause it's your own fault for mollycoddlin' him all these years. Tom's been a load on my mind for long enough, and if it hadn't been for your always takin' his side, he'd have gone down the mine since June when he graduated. By Jaysus, he would have, just like his brother Jim."

Having left the kitchen, Elizabeth didn't hear all the tirade—or wish to hear it. Besides, she knew that her husband was just letting off steam.

A few moments later, Tom appeared with an improvised sling on his right arm, a bandana provided by his mother.

Jim immediately greeted his brother, with a bright smile. "Where were you last night, Tom?"

"Out," Tom replied, using Jim's word as he sat down at the table.

"'Out?' Jim repeated with a grin. "Where's out?"

"Up the hill."

"How'd you hurt your arm?"

"I stumbled in the dark comin' down," Tom said, averting his eyes.

During this interrogation, John glowered at his middle son, but in silence.

"What were you doin' up there in the dark anyway?" Jim asked.

"I wasn't doin' anything," Tom insisted, meeting his brother's eyes.

"Nothin'?" Jim asked.

"Yeah, that's what I just said."

"You weren't with someone?"

"No."

"You were up there alone?"

"I just said so."

"You sure you weren't makin' out with Nola Henze?"

"No, I wasn't."

"Hasn't Mr. Henze offered to make you his business partner?"

"You kiddin'?"

"For heaven's sake, Jim, do let him eat his breakfast!" Elizabeth said as she suddenly appeared in the kitchen. "Tom, will you be going to work today?"

"Yeah, sure I will, Mom," Tom said.

"You shouldn't be climbing the hill in the dark," Elizabeth said, drawing the venom of her husband's unspoken wrath. "When a son of mine comes home hurt, it's my duty to find out what's happened to him."

"What do you want me to say, Mom?" Tom said, conscious that she was trying to appease his father. "I just said that I fell comin' down the hill, so it was only an accident."

"Were you alone?" Elizabeth asked, unwittingly repeating Jim's question.

"Yeah, that's what I just said."

"It would be easier to speak with the wall!" Elizabeth exclaimed.

When John and Jim left for the mine, Tom quickly ate his breakfast, then dashed upstairs to put on his jacket, which normally took but a moment, but this time took a full minute. At ten to seven, he called good-bye to his mother and loped up Main Street, only his left arm cleaving the air. He paused to look back at the black column of smoke rising from the mine at the far end of Main Street, where a light breeze out of the northeast was blowing it to the southwest. The eastern horizon was a pale blue with the sun slanting over the Appalachians.

Reaching Henze's Grocery Store, Tom saw that Fred had already brought in the newspaper bundles, along with the crates of milk from the dairy and the bread cartons from the bakery.

*Nola must have told her father I had an accident,* Tom thought as he stepped into the store.

"Hiya, Tom, I didn't expect to see you today," Fred said without turning from unpacking a carton of evaporated milk and placing the cans in the shelf behind the register. "Nola says you hurt your arm?"

"Just bruised it, Mr.—er—Fred," Tom replied, grinning. He went to the back of the store for his apron and took more than a minute to put it on too.

When Tom reappeared, Fred said, "Tom, do you wanna work

the cash register today, which might make it easier for your arm, doncha think?"

"Thanks, Mr.—er—Fred, but I'll be all right," Tom insisted.

"Nice weather we've been havin'. So I guess it's Indian summer."

"Yeah, I guess so. Last night I could see stars down to the fifth magnitude."

"That so?" Fred responded absently. "Have you seen the paper this mornin'?"

"Something about the war over in Europe, I suppose?"

"Yeah. You boys will be over there before you can say Jack Robinson, if we don't watch out. Tom, what do you think about the war?"

"I never thought about it."

"We were the same last time," Fred said. "I was a kid then, too young to know much, but running around like a crazy galoot and—bingo!—I found myself in khaki. We were all shipped over to Europe like a boatload of cattle, only they treat cattle better. We came home a sadder, wiser bunch—those that did come back. I was glad to be among the living."

"Fred, after the last time, do you really think that we'll fight over in Europe?" Tom asked.

"You bet we will. Look at this son-of-a-bitch Roosevelt inviting the king and queen of England to have tea at Hyde Park."

"But isn't Europe three thousand miles away?"

"It wasn't too far last time. Besides, I don't have a bone to pick with the Germans, as my grandfather was born over there. Grandpappy used to call Germany *Die Vaterland*, which means the Fatherland."

"I'd love to see Europe."

"There's better ways to see Europe than bein' shot at," Fred said with a dismissive laugh.

"Did you get to see anything of Europe when you were over there?"

"We landed at a place called Le Harve, which in French means 'the harbor,' but there wasn't much to see there, less you call docks, gantry cranes, and warehouses somethin' to see. As soon as we got off the boat, this Frog picked my pocket, cleaning me out. But it didn't matter much, 'cause there was nothin' to spend money on anyway."

"Did you see Paris, Mr.—er—Fred?"

"I sure did!"

"Did you like Paris?"

"It's bigger than Le Harve, with a lot more Frogs. But gimme Ridgeton any day."

"Still, Europe must be a great place to learn a foreign language, without havin' to study a grammar book."

"I suppose it is, but Poppy didn't want Grandpappy to teach me German. Grandpappy used to teach me a few words, but Poppy told him, 'I want Fred to speak English, 'cause he was born an American.' That's what Poppy told him."

"Of course, I'd need a lot of money to learn a foreign language in Europe."

"I suppose you would, Tom, but I was damn glad to get back home," Fred said. "That's the shame of the war, you see. Some boys don't come home and marry their sweethearts, have a family, and make something of themselves. One war was enough for me—more than enough!—*merci beaucoup, Mam-wah-selle from Ar-min-teers!*"

"I suppose you're right, Fred," Tom said. "But I'm not going to worry about the war, because it's been going on in Europe for almost two years now, and it's mostly been talkin', not fightin'. Do you think that maybe we've gotten too civilized for war?"

"Don't you believe that, Tom. The day'll come when no man's

left to shoot another, an' if he don't have a rifle, he'll use a club or his bare fists, but fight he must."

"Fred, did you find the war very exciting?"

"Tom, I'm too old for that kind of excitement!" Fred exclaimed, laughing. "Maybe, once you get older, you get a bit wiser too."

All morning Tom rang the cash register with his left hand, while housewives made no fuss in doing the bagging, asking Tom about his arm. At noon Fred relieved Tom, who took a roast beef sandwich and a half pint of chocolate milk from the refrigerator, then went outside to eat in the backyard. All morning Tom had wondered why Nola hadn't come down into the store, thinking she must be offended by his trying to kiss her the night before. When he'd finished, he heard the screen door upstairs slam and looked up.

"How's your arm feel today, Tom?" Nola asked, leaning over the rail.

"It's all right," Tom replied, smiling.

"How's my father been today?"

"Same as ever."

"What's his mood like?"

"I didn't ask him."

"Are you busy?"

"I'm always busy—doin' nothin'!"

"Would you like to go for a picnic?"

"I've just eaten."

"Aren't you always hungry?"

"That's true!" Tom confessed, grinning.

"What do you say we have a picnic?"

"It's your funeral!"

A few minutes later, Nola appeared from the back door, carrying with her a brown paper bag. "We're all set!" she brightly announced.

Wincing with pain, Tom stood up but said nothing.

"We'll have a picnic up on the hill," Nola said.

Tom followed her up the alley into the bright sunlight of Main Street. Suddenly she so abruptly stopped that he almost bumped into her.

"Tom, if you don't wish to go, just say so!" Nola exclaimed, her blue eyes flashing.

"Didn't I just say I would?" Tom asked, looking hurt.

"Does that mean you do? Because if you don't, let's call it off!"

"What did your father say?" Tom asked, ignoring her ultimatum.

"Nothing!" Nola said. "Tom, what's got into you?"

"Never mind. Besides, it doesn't matter."

"What doesn't matter?"

"Nola, will you stop bossin' me around!"

Nola raised her voice. "You think I'm bossy?"

"Yes, you are!"

"Don't you think you're being very silly?"

"No, I don't think I am."

"You're getting on my nerves!"

"Then don't lead me around by the nose!"

She held up her hand. "I could hit you!"

"Go ahead. It would be better than this bickerin'!"

Nola shrugged, and they continued walking in silence. Past Preston's Mobil Station, they started to climb the hill, Tom going first. Halfway up he stopped and, turning to her, said, "Nola, do you really want to know a jerk like me?"

"Tom, you're not a jerk," she replied, looking closely into his brown eyes. "Besides, you were perfectly right."

"How do you figure that?"

"Well, isn't the boy the one to do the chasing?" Nola asked, smiling brightly.

"So, you don't think I'm a jerk?" Tom asked, his brow creased.

"Tom, don't humble yourself."

"You don't think me egotistical either?"

"No, not particularly."

"There's nothing wrong with me?"

"I'm sure that nothing is wrong with you."

"So I'm not even selfish?"

"You don't believe a word you're saying!" Nola exclaimed with her light laugh.

"Nola, you're the only girl who's ever listened to me or taken me seriously," Tom confessed, staring into her blue eyes.

"What about your sister, Sarah?"

"She doesn't count."

"Do you find it difficult to express your feelings?"

"Yes, but Nola, you understand me."

"I do try, believe me!" Nola exclaimed with a chuckle.

When they reached the summit, they looked down on the gray rooftops of Ridgeton, bathed in afternoon sunlight. Stooping, Tom picked up a stone from the grass and turned it from side to side, examining it closely. "I used to carry a stone like this one to school when I was a kid," he said. "Whenever I felt frustrated because I couldn't understand something, I'd touch it. It had mica flecks like this one. You know, sometimes I wanted to throw the stone through the school window, just to see the reaction on the kids' faces."

"But, Tom, you didn't do it. You decided it would be better to suppress your own feelings than to throw the stone. But I wouldn't have thrown the stone either. Tom, being alone too much isn't good, because we have to live our lives with other people according to society's rules, which benefit everyone. Do you see that, Tom?"

Tom did not reply, but momentarily balancing himself, he threw the stone with his left hand and watched it strike the hillside far below.

"Tom, you shouldn't throw stones, not even with your good arm," Nola chided him.

"I've got to practice with my left arm, just in case I lose the use of my right," Tom insisted, gazing into her sparkling eyes.

"Don't kid yourself, Tom!"

"Why am I kiddin' myself?" he asked, frowning.

"Because you're just like you were in school, when you wished to throw a stone through the window."

"Why didn't I do it, then?"

"Because that wasn't in your nature."

"Yeah, I guess I just like to ask a lot of silly questions."

"Asking a lot of questions is better, for you might get some answers," Nola said.

"What has asking a lot of questions done for me?" Tom lamented. "Just look at me. I'm all set for life workin' in the grocery store, and the boss's daughter is takin' me out to lunch."

"And paying for the privilege!" Nola exclaimed, laughing in spite of herself. "By the way, how many boss's daughters have you dated?"

"None, besides you."

"That's what I thought, but don't call my father The Boss, because he won't like it."

"That's why I call him The Boss,'" Tom said with a grin.

"How come I've never heard you call him that?"

"Because I never would to his face."

"Why do you say it to me then?"

"Because I think of you as The Boss's daughter."

"I see!" Nola said with a far-off gaze, sitting down in the deep grass, facing Tom. She took a peanut butter and jelly sandwich from the bag and gave it to him, saying, "Now, Tom, tell me all you know about girls."

"I don't know anything about girls!" Tom confessed, blushing.

"That's what I thought." Nola giggled.

"Don't rub it in!" Tom said, grinning.

"Your sister must have told you something about girls?"

"That's different." Tom said, shrugging his shoulders.

"I suppose it is."

"Nola, why do you think I don't have a girlfriend?" Tom asked.

"I guess you don't want one," Nola said, studying his eyes.

"Nola, you're different from any girl I've ever known. I don't have to hide my feelings from you."

"Why should you want to hide them?"

"Is there something wrong with our being together?"

"Why should that be wrong?" Nola asked with a look of surprise.

"Nola, you could go out with any guy you wished."

"I believe I've done that already!" she exclaimed, followed by her light laugh.

"Do you remember who you were with when *King Kong* was playing at the Alhambra when you pretended not to notice me?"

"Perhaps I didn't notice you!"

"You were with Dave Coulton."

"Then I didn't notice you!" Nola laughed.

"What did you think about me at first?"

"What do you mean, *think* about you?"

"Did you think me different?"

"I guess I did, but when you started working at the store, you seemed so self-possessed."

"And here I thought you were ignoring me!"

"But why should I ignore you?"

"Because you didn't want to have to lower your social status," Tom said as he looked across into the blue ranges.

"No, Tom, that wasn't it at all. You see, I didn't really know you all that well."

"Except as the joker who'd helped you with your homework!"

"Tom, you won't believe me, but I admired you even before then."

"Admired me for what?"

"I admired your intensity when you were doing something."

"Let's forget about me!"

They ate their sandwiches, while looking down over the rooftops of Ridgeton bathed in the afternoon sunlight.

"Nola, I do like being with you," Tom said, looking at her askance.

"What if I said that I didn't?" Nola asked teasingly.

Tom smiled. "Then I'd have to say that you don't appreciate me."

"What don't I appreciate about you?"

"How I feel about you."

"Do you want an egg salad sandwich?" she asked.

"Is that your answer to my question?"

"You didn't ask me a question. In fact, I asked you one."

"I guess I'm still hungry," Tom said, looking sheepish.

"Are you always hungry?" Nola asked as she fished out the egg salad sandwich and gave it to him, saying, "Perhaps you should have eaten this one first?"

"It's goin' to the same place."

"Does your arm feel any better?" Nola asked, unwrapping her own sandwich.

"It feels okay," Tom replied, before quickly demolishing the sandwich with a few bites. Then he unzipped his jacket and tried to extricate his left arm.

"Here, let me help you," Nola said. "Won't you feel chilly wearing only your T-shirt?"

"I like to feel the warmth of the sun. Today it feels just like Indian summer." Tom lay back in the grass, his head propped up by his left arm. "Nola, do you think I'm feedin' you a line?"

"That's the last thing I expected to hear you say! But then, I don't really know what to expect from you."

"Why do you say that?"

"Well, yesterday I overheard you talking about the war with my father."

"Your father hasn't forgotten the last war."

"Why do you say that?"

"Because, I guess, it's only the dead who forget."

"Don't be morbid!" Nola exclaimed, a shiver passing along her spine.

"If we get involved in this war, I'll probably get knocked off," Tom said, sitting up, his head lower than his shoulders.

"I should hope not!" Nola declared with a dismissive laugh. Then quietly, she added, "If we enter this war, it will upset everybody's plans."

"When you're killed, that's the end of your plans."

"Please don't say that, Tom. Besides, not many of our boys got killed last time."

"Maybe fifty thousand," Tom said, turning to stare into her blue eyes. "Does anybody ever think of them now? If they'd lived, they might be sitting behind big desks now, the captains of industry. But someone else got their jobs, along with their dreams of marryin' their sweethearts and raisin' their own families, which came to nothing. Do you know what I think? I think that wars are caused by ignorant politicians who come to believe their own lies, because they won't have to do any of the fightin' anyway."

"Tom, maybe there really aren't any answers."

"Then why do the politicians act as if there are? The war's stupid, too, and nobody can explain it, except maybe in a hundred years when some historian will prove that it was all a big mistake. For there are no winners or losers, because even the winners are losers, if you know what I mean."

"Tom, I never heard you speak so bitterly about the war," Nola said. "Didn't you tell my father that you didn't know much about the war, not even from the newspaper?"

"Don't you see, Nola? If we get involved in the war, it'll be the same as last time. The only difference will be that another generation has passed, and people have forgotten and started bein' patriotic because the last war has become a hazy memory. Nola, do you mind if I take off my shirt?" He noticed her blue eyes sparkling in the sunlight.

"I don't mind, Tom."

"I just thought you might," Tom said, grinning sheepishly as he pulled off his T-shirt, lay back on the grass, and closed his eyes.

"Nola, am I too skinny?" Tom opened his eyes and turned to her.

"Did I say that?" Nola asked, a smile on her lips.

"No, but you think so, don't you?"

"Yes, I do," Nola confessed, laughing.

"Nola, when did you first find out how you felt about me?" Tom asked in halting words.

"Longer than you're aware!"

"How long?"

"When you first came to work in the store."

"Why didn't you tell me?"

"Do girls tell boys such things?" Nola asked with a mischievous smile. "Besides, I had the distinct impression that you didn't want to become involved."

"Whaddya mean?"

"I believe that my meaning's perfectly clear—if impossible to explain to you."

"Do you think me antisocial?" Tom asked, frowning.

"No, not antisocial but self-sufficient."

"Don't you mean egotistical?"

"I said self-sufficient. You were so self-absorbed in whatever it was you were doing with your nose in a book! Anyway, I thought you were different."

"Different?" Tom asked with pain in his voice.

"I mean different from the other boys. You were interested in so many things, and I was always interested in what you might say. Other boys were more assertive, but you always treated me with respect."

"I don't blame girls for getting upset when a guy treats them like a jerk," Tom said. "Because the way some guys treat girls revolts me. I wouldn't want my sister treated like that. I think girls put up with a lot."

"Is that what Sarah told you?"

"I guess she did!" Tom said, laughing. "But it's exactly how I feel myself."

"What kind of girls attract you?"

"One who respects herself and doesn't look like some movie star."

"That lets me off!" Nola exclaimed as she sat up, looking over the Appalachian ranges to the west, where high cirrus clouds with long wispy strands were veiling the sky.

"Nola, I feel about girls just like any other guy," Tom confessed, sitting up and hunching over to look askance at the side of her face, where her golden hair almost reached her shoulders. "Just looking at a beautiful girl can keep me awake for most of the night. But I don't want to feel lousy or be degraded by going to a prostitute just to lose my virginity. I would like to fall in love with some girl who loves me without anything cheap or shameful. I'll behave respectfully toward her because I want her to respect me without thinkin' I'm only interested in one thing."

"Tom, please don't go on!" Nola exclaimed, laughing in spite of herself.

"I'll shut up then!" Tom said, lying on his back in the deep grass and closing his eyes, wondering why he'd told her so much about himself.

A moment later Tom opened his eyes and saw that Nola was gone. Sitting up, he saw that she was standing on a rock that jutted above the hillside. She was precariously poised, with her slim figure silhouetted in the westering sunlight. Slowly Tom pulled himself to his feet and stepped behind her, where he slipped his left arm around her waist, drawing her close.

"Nola, what would my life be without you?" he whispered in her ear.

Nola did not respond, possessed by her own thoughts as she gazed over the blue Appalachians.

"Nola, do I have to get down on my knees to prove that I love you?" Tom asked, as he gently tightened his grip.

"Tom, don't act as if you're not worth knowing," Nola said as she turned around and faced him.

"Maybe you don't feel like I do," Tom said, a wry smile on his lips.

"Do you really believe that, Tom?"

"So, I'm not the jerk you think I am?"

"Don't say that, Tom," she protested. "You're just like any other boy."

"Whaddya mean?"

"You want to be happy just as much as they do."

"Nola, I'd like to live the rest of my life without my T-shirt."

"Won't you catch pneumonia?" she asked as Tom lifted her into the air with his left arm and spun around above the hillside before setting her down again.

"Nola, will you scratch my back?" he asked, grinning.

"Tom, what if I'd fallen?"

"Never fear, Tom's here!" he exclaimed, laughing at the danger as he put on his T-shirt and jacket with Nola's help.

Halfway down the hill, Tom stopped and faced Nola. Clouds were being driven by the wind, far above the earth.

"Nola, nothing is going to come between us," Tom said, stooping to pluck a seed stalk, which he stuck between his front teeth.

"Tom, my father says we're going into this war," she said, looking off to the hills.

"Yeah, I know, but all this talk of war is crazy. After the last one, why would anyone want to go over to fight in Europe again?"

"Then why should we get involved? Besides, haven't the Europeans always fought wars?"

"Yeah, I guess they have. My dad says that a war would be good for business; it would get us out of the Great Depression."

"That idea's crazy!" Nola exclaimed.

"Maybe so, but my father says that the capitalists are the bad guys. Dad says the English and the Germans can settle their differences if they get together like the guys at Grogh's and Rathskeller's. If they'd meet halfway, they could work out their differences and become good friends. And maybe if the English and Germans spoke the same language, there wouldn't be the problem. But the Germans have elected this crackpot Hitler, who blames the Jews for Germany's defeat during the First World War, sayin' that the Jews made all the money, so he's come to reclaim Germany's national honor."

"Maybe we should think of the Civil War as stupid like that too," she said. "But we don't think of it as stupid. If we did, we wouldn't have put up a statue of a Union soldier outside the post office in Main Street."

"Nola, evil hasn't just come into the world," Tom said. "Besides, the Civil War was so long ago that we've romanticized it, sayin' that it was a war to free the slaves. But the historians don't all agree on that. So maybe there were no victors. Maybe it's only a question of how much you've learned to hate—how many people you wish to kill."

"Tom, I don't think that we should get involved in another war or that you should have to go," she said in a level voice.

"Nola, I just wish they'd use the wasted lives and the lost money for the benefit of humankind. So everyone could get an education and make something of themselves. Maybe I'd raise better crops or breed cows that give more milk. But I won't be able to do any of that if I don't get an education or am sent off to fight in a war that no one believes in."

"I do hope that you're not sent to the war in Europe, so that you can do what you wish," Nola said in a confident tone.

"If we go to war, I'll be the first, because I'll volunteer. If I come back, I'll march down Main Street behind the flag, feelin' stupid after seein' all that death and destruction."

"Don't say that, Tom." Nola pressed her hands to her ears.

"But maybe your father's wrong," Tom said. "Maybe there won't be a war, so that I won't have to go."

"Tell me what you just said to me?"

"What was that?" Tom asked, surprised.

"Didn't you tell me that you love me?" Nola asked, a smile on her lips.

Tom's brows shot up as he asked, "What were you doing the first time you realized you loved me?"

"You'll laugh!"

"I promise I won't."

"I was hanging the laundry on the line. You were seated on a milk crate, having lunch in the backyard. After I'd finished, I went inside but stayed behind the screen door, watching you. You were hunched over, scratching the ground with a stick. You hair looked disheveled, and you looked very thin. At that moment, I became angry with myself for feeling as I did."

"Why did you feel angry?"

"I felt like a fool! Until then, I'd hardly thought of you and wished to disown my feelings. It was torture, believe me!"

"Why do you say that?"

"Because you were so oblivious! You didn't even know that you were driving me mad."

"Nola, I only wish I could tell you how I feel about you."

"You don't have to, because I'm so afraid for our future."

"Don't worry about that." Tom put his arm around her, drawing her close. "Whatever happens, our future will always be happy and bright."

She rested her head against Tom's heart. "The future will be ours if only we can be together," she said, looking up at his face.

"I love you, Nola," Tom said and kissed her lips.

It was late summer, and the lush, green grass was growing on the hill where milkweed pods had burst, spewing their feathery parachutes far and wide. Late summer had come, to be followed by fall and winter, which would bring death's rattle, covering the ground with a blanket of snow, as the earth completed its cycle. From time immemorial, the course of young love has been foretold in the heavens, but youth is oblivious, and old age and death seem far off. Would that they could have fulfilled their dream!

# CHAPTER 7

● ● ● ● ● ● ● ● ● ● ● ● ● ● ● ● ● ● ● ● ● ● ● ● ● ● ● ● ● ● ●

"YESTERDAY, DECEMBER 7, 1941—a date which will live in infamy—the United States of America was suddenly and deliberately attacked by naval and air forces of the Empire of Japan."

So spoke President Roosevelt before a joint session of Congress when he declared war on the emperor of Japan and on Adolf Hitler of Germany. The boys of Ridgeton had not wished to go to war, but they knew what they must do. The nation had sought God's protection, for their lives had been spun on a simpler theme, but now they had to don the armor of Achilles. Aroused, a fierce indignation burned in the heart of the Great Republic.

The long sleep of youth ended that Sunday morning, as Phoebus Apollo had leapt from the Atlantic waves, casting his bright beams on the Appalachians as he has from time immemorial, before lighting the Great Plains and the Rocky Mountains and shining on the Pacific Ocean. Drums were being beaten to arouse dawdling youth, who were ready to march with a bright gleam in their eyes, for the Old World, having succumbed to evil, was in its death throes.

Youth's flesh burned with the light that was in its bones.

Hearing the drumbeat, Tom Blaine answered his country's call, for he was eager to slay the dragon that lurked in the depths of night. The age-old war mania had been revived and burned in the minds of men, white as the noonday sun on the dusty roads of summer. Already their throats were parched with an unslakable thirst, and their eyes burned like hot coals in their sockets. Ridgeton had never seen such excitement, not since the last war had been declared. Unthinking, the boys had joined up, amid laughter and coarse jokes, ahead of them the dry mouth and the dusty road.

No different from the others, Tom had said to himself, *I must join up and do my part.* His decision was an easy one, for already it had been made for him half the world away, in a place he'd never heard of called Pearl Harbor. All he had to do was to step into the ranks.

"Nola, I hope you won't ever forget me," Tom said as they stood again on the hill, despite winter's biting cold when the days were short and the sun was already far down in the west, and soon the bright stars would be shining over Ridgeton.

"Tom, how could I forget you?" Nola asked. "Wasn't it up here on the hill that we first confessed our love for each other? This hill has been our world."

"Yeah, the only spot on earth that is sacred to me, since I found you," Tom confessed, his eyes locking on hers.

"I know that in your heart you'll never leave this hill, nor will I."

"I've loved you because you accept me as I am."

"My only regret, Tom, is that you won't be starting at Lafayette College in January. Education has meant so much to you, and now that you've won a scholarship, it's a pity that you won't be able to go."

"As soon as I come back, I'll go," Tom said. "Anyway, who would have thought that I'd get a scholarship?"

"Tom, you earned it. I only wish that you didn't have to go to war."

"Every guy's enlisted. So I'd look like a slouch if I waited to be drafted."

"But why can't the war wait till you've finished college?" Nola knew the answer.

"I'm leavin' tomorrow for Camp Dix in New Jersey," Tom said as if he hadn't told her a hundred times already. "When I've finished boot camp, I'll get a pass and come home to Ridgeton before being shipped overseas. Jim's joined the Marines, and Sarah joined the WACs, leavin' only Luke at home. Doncha see, Nola? That's why I have to go, even though I hate having to leave you."

"I'll keep an eagle eye on the mailbox, waiting to hear from you," Nola said as she smiled, her voice optimistic.

Fumbling in his pants pocket, Tom produced a small box and opened it.

"Tom, it's lovely!" Nola exclaimed as tears welled in her eyes.

"I want us to be married right away," he said as he put the ring on her finger.

"But, Tom?"

"What's the matter, Nola?" Tom said, frowning.

"Tom, let's be engaged for a while."

"What for, Nola? I want to marry you now, not later."

"Tom, let's be engaged for a while first."

"Nola, don't you wish to marry me?"

"Yes, Tom, I do, but not now. Besides, at the moment, I can't think straight."

"We don't have any time to think." Tom put his arms around her and kissed her as if that would make her change her mind.

"Tom, where did you get the money to buy the ring?"

"Jim loaned it to me," he confessed quietly. "I've spoken with my mother, and she wants you to come to dinner tonight so that we can celebrate. Mom wants your mom and dad to come."

"My mother won't come, and Dad won't come without her."

"Doesn't your mother like me?"

"My mother doesn't know you, Tom."

"You know, I haven't seen your mother in years," Tom said in a quiet voice as if he were thinking aloud.

"Five years, in fact, Tom. That's how long my mother's kept to her room."

"Is something the matter with her?"

"Not exactly."

"What is it, then? Can't she walk?"

"Yes, but she rarely does."

"What's wrong with her then?"

"She's afraid that something might happen to her, so she won't go out."

"Like what?"

"I'm not quite sure."

"Have you asked her?"

"I've given up asking."

"Did something happen to her?"

"Yes, she fainted on the bus."

"When was that?"

"Five years ago when she visited Burt and Lucy in Wilkes-Barre."

"Was she hurt?"

"No, but when she got home, she refused to leave the house."

"Why?"

"From embarrassment, I suppose."

"Is that what she said?"

"No, she's never said anything to me."

"Have you asked her?"

"No. I've told you, I've stopped asking her."

That evening before dinner, John Blaine marched his middle son into the front parlor, a room that was rarely used, save by Elizabeth when she entertained the Reverend Stoppelmoor on his semiannual pastoral visits. Tom knew that his father wanted to speak with him before he went to boot camp. He also was aware that words did not come easily to his father. But the time for fatherly counsel had come.

John stood on the hearth rug with his back to the fire, clasping his hands behind him while his son stood on his mother's favorite Axminster rug, contemplating its floral design.

"Tom, a good many years ago I was in the exact same position you're in now, and I was just your age," John said with a full head of steam. "But not bein' a scholar like yourself, I didn't know half of what you now know. You see, I went the way the wind blows. Fortunately I didn't go far away, 'cause I'd found the love of a good woman. I expect you feel much the same way as I did back then, since you've become engaged. You haven't allowed yourself much time to sow your wild oats, as Jim tells me. In that case, you must be serious, and this is for keeps.

"Mind you, I think that Nola is a fine, levelheaded girl, but you've got a bed of nails with her ol' lady. Grace Henze is the proudest and most stuck-up woman that a man can meet, and I'm sure that she will have given her daughter a piece of her mind if she hasn't done so already. I don't dislike Fred Henze, but he takes his marchin' orders from his wife. I don't suppose that either of them will be coming to dinner tonight, even though your mother invited them."

"Nola says that they won't come," Tom replied.

"Well, there you have it!" John said. "And your mother tells me that you wish to be married right away?"

"I do, Dad, but Nola wants us to be engaged for a while."

"What's all the rush around?"

"Dad, if I'm killed, I'll have never known what it is to love a woman."

"Doncha love her now?" John asked.

"Dad, I mean conjugal relations," Tom said, blushing.

"Then, say so!"

"Dad, I was afraid that if I got killed, I'd have never known what—"

"Of course you were afraid. Back then we were all afraid, but we did what we had to do, like you're doin' now. None of us had the time to think, same as you don't now. Before I married your mother, I spent every dollar as fast as I got it. I was seventeen, cuttin' coal seams, borin' into the earth like a mole. Except I wasn't a mole, but a human being with the light of reason in my noodle. When your mother and I got married, she tried to educate me as best she could—teachin' me that there were some things in this world that weren't workin' down a coal mine. Something I hadn't known about and couldn't imagine."

Tom stared at his mother's Axminster rug as his father spoke.

"So, when the war came, I was just as scared as you are now. I could kick myself for my lack of ambition, but I was a steady worker who provided for your mother and our kids, keepin' little for myself, save the few bucks she gave me on Friday. Everything was for the good of the family, and I have no regrets."

Tom looked up into his father's gray eyes. He saw that they were filled with formless ideas, swirling around as if in a dust storm.

"Jim's a fine boy. So's Luke. And Sarah's a good girl. But sometimes it's hard to see your own blessings that are starin' you right in the face. I know that you always thought of your ol' man as bein' hardest on you, 'cause of your desire for an education. But, Tom, I'm proud of you, and I don't want you goin' off without your father's blessin'. You should have gone to college, now that you've got a scholarship, even though you'll soon be drafted anyway.

"Another thing, I'm proud as hell that you dug your heels in and refused to go down the mine, 'cause it's done nothin' for me. Soon I'll be put out to pasture. So don't think that if I had my time to live over again, I wouldn't make some changes. My lungs are shot, too, but as yet I haven't told your mother. I'm just an old nag, ready for the pasture. And my back ain't good. It's been hurtin' me. So it's too late for me, Tom."

"Don't say that, Dad," Tom protested, knowing that his father always ended up talking about himself.

"Tom, when you get right down to it, there ain't nothing that I can say." John clasped his middle son in his arms and gave him a bear hug.

Elizabeth served Tom's favorite dinner that night: roast lamb with baked potatoes and peas. Sarah came from the WACs in Philadelphia, bringing her boyfriend, Dan Willoughby. Nola made a final appeal to her mother, saying that it would be the first time that they'd had a meal together as an engaged couple. To guarantee Nola's appearance and strengthen her resolve, Tom went to the store to bring her home. Outside the kitchen door, he kissed her for good luck.

Just then, Jim opened the kitchen door and exclaimed, "I just caught 'em canoodlin'!"

"Thanks a lot, Jim!" Tom cried, his face as red as a beet.

Nola was demure, however, smiling and unfazed at all this. She knew that Jim's joke wasn't at her expense. When they were all seated, John produced a bottle of wine that he'd just bought at Grogh's Tavern and filled their glasses to toast the happy couple, saying, "May you always be as happy as you are now, and may you both live to be as old as Methuselah!"

"And may they all return safely from the war," Elizabeth added as she raised her glass.

"I'll drink to that, Mrs. Blaine!" Dan Willoughby exclaimed, raising his glass, a light in his gray eyes.

After finishing with apple pie for dessert, Luke produced a letter his French high school teacher had given him from a girl in France who sought a pen pal in America. "Sarah," he said, "can you translate this letter for me?"

"Translate it yourself, since you're studying French," Sarah said, teasing him.

"Are you crazy, Sarah?" Luke protested. "Why can't she write in English?"

"Oh, give me the letter!" Sarah said amid general amusement.

"How did she mail a letter out of France?" Dan asked.

"It's probably from the unoccupied zone," Tom said.

"Tom always has the answer to every question," Nola said, giving her intended a gentle poke.

"Sure I do!" Tom blushed, having become the focus of attention.

"Sarah, pay no attention to their shenanigans, and get on with the letter," John said.

"'*Je viens d'avoir votre adresse par mon professeur d'Anglais et je m'empresse de vous écrire,*'" Sarah began to read.

"I'm lost already!" John boomed, obviously proud of his daughter.

"What does it mean?" Luke asked.

"The French girl has gotten your letter from her English teacher and writes to you," Sarah said.

"Is that what she said, then?" John asked.

"Yes, Daddy, that's what it means in French," Sarah explained with a benevolent smile.

"Then I stand corrected. Sarah, do go on."

"'*Mon nom est Suzanne Moulin,*'" Sarah continued.

"'Moulin'?" Tom said. "Doesn't that mean 'mill'?"

"Yes, it does, just like the Moulin Rouge," Sarah replied.

"Don't you think that Suzanne is a lovely name?" Nola said.

"Get on with the letter, love," John said, impatient with the interruptions. "I find that I like the sound of French, even though I don't understand it."

"French is a very musical language," Elizabeth said.

"Do go on with it, love," John added.

"'J'ai seize ans. Je suis en pension à Evreux, mais j'habite à Couches,'" Sarah said.

"What's she sayin' now?" Luke asked.

"Tom, if they ship you to France, all the French you'll need is Coo-shay-voo aveck mwah se swar," Jim said.

"Jim, keep your breath to cool your porridge!" Elizabeth said, for she remembered enough French to know that his comment was unseemly.

"Mother, please ignore Jim," Sarah said, knowing her brother only too well.

"Sarah, will you get on with the letter," John said again, scowling at his eldest son.

"Well, Suzanne lives in a boarding house in the town of Evreux, but her hometown is Couches, which is evidently close by," Sarah explained.

"Evroo?" Jim said contemptuously. "Why don't the French speak a language we can understand?"

"I suppose, Jim, you mean a universal language, like Esperanto?" Dan said.

"Naw, I think that all these foreigners should speak English, instead of talkin' gibberish," Jim insisted.

"Sarah, pay no attention to your eldest brother and get on with the letter," John said again.

"'Evreux est à cent kilometres de Paris, capitale de la France,'"

Sarah read. "*'Je vais vous faire un petit portrait de moi et plus tard je vous enverrai ma photo.'* Translated, that means that Evreux is one hundred kilometers from Paris, the capital of France. And soon she'll send you her photo."

"Luke, I'd wait till she sends it, just to see what she looks like, in case she's a dog," Jim advised.

"That's quite enough, Jim!" Elizabeth said amid general laughter.

"Go on, Sarah, let's hear the rest of it." John looked sternly at his eldest son.

"Luke, you won't have to wait to find out what Suzanne looks like, as she describes herself," Sarah said. "*'J'ai les cheveux blond cendré, et j'ai une matte relevé sur la tête en forme de diadème. J'ai les yeux bleus.'* Translated, that means she's got ash-blonde hair, which is plaited in a diadem, and blue eyes. She's taking a secretarial course, wishing to become a secretary. Let me see, what else?"

"Go on, Sarah, and read it all in French," John proudly urged her. "I find French music to my ears."

"*'J'aime beaucoup la musique. Mes choses préféres sont le cinéma, et la musique. En classe j'aime beaucoup étudier la Geographie, l'Histoire, et l'Anglais.'* She goes on to say that she likes movies, music, and her favorite subjects are geography, history, and English. Luke, do try to write to her in French."

"Why can't she write to me in English?" he protested.

"Actually she does, Luke." Sarah had looked ahead.

"I've no doubt whatever that she speaks better English than we do," Elizabeth said. "In Europe, you see, they're way ahead of us in teaching foreign languages."

"Maybe Suzanne and I have that much in common," Jim wisecracked.

"Jim, I'll be the judge of that!" John said.

"Well, here goes!" Sarah exclaimed, laughing. "'I have a sister.

His name is Marguerite. But I have not brother, at my great regret. My father and mother are grocer. Have you brother and sister? Couches is a little town of three thousand inhabitants. How many inhabitants in Ridgeton? Evreux is a town of twenty thousand inhabitants. Have you traveled in America? I do not traveled very much in France. I have go to Paris and some towns in France. Where is exactly Ridgeton? In the Atlantique coast? Today the weather is fine. There was the ice this morning and it was cold, but the sun shines. I do not like the cold weather, but I like very much when the weather is very hot in summer. I hope received your letter soon. My kindest regards to you, Suzanne. P.S.: *Ne tardez trop s'il vous plaît à m'écrire.'*"

"What's that last part mean, Sarah?" Jim asked.

"It means 'Write soon!'"

"All those words, just to say that?" Jim asked.

"Okay, let me translate," Sarah replied, grimacing at her eldest brother. "'Please do not hesitate to write to me.' Does that sound better, Jim?"

"Well, if you ask me it sounds more polite than 'Write soon'!" John said.

At midnight, Tom kissed Nola good-bye at the foot of the stairs behind the grocery store. Nola promised not to see him off at ten-to-seven the following morning.

But she found it impossible to keep that promise. At 6:45 she suddenly appeared, and they embraced and kissed before the statue of the Union rifleman outside the post office on Main Street. Tears welled in their eyes, and they were oblivious to the small group of people who'd come to see the boys off, to shake their hands and give them bear hugs or back slaps amid the general laughter.

The recruits boarded the Greyhound bus, and it moved down Main Street amid the acrid fumes, passing Henze's Grocery Store and the Preston Mobil Station on the edge of town. Tom craned his neck to peer up at the snow-covered hill, which seemed to belong more to the sky than to the earth. Though he was surrounded by young men he had grown up with, Tom felt very much alone—lonelier than he'd ever felt before.

Nola's onetime boyfriend, Dave Coulton, sat across the aisle from him. Impulsively Nola had kissed Dave good-bye after she'd kissed Tom; he could still see the smudge of her lipstick on his cheek. Vince Doerlinger, whose father owned the bakery, sat next to Tom, and behind him was Jim's buddy "Doc" Hodges, who'd gone down Smedwick's Coal Mine along with him. All the boys had been swept up in the general excitement, for they'd all enlisted without waiting to be drafted.

"Tom, you got any idea when we'll arrive over there?" Jim Seramba called to him from a couple of seats ahead.

"I think we'll get there in a couple of hours," Tom replied.

"They say that Dan Willoughby's joined the navy. Is it true?" Jim asked.

"Yeah, he did, and my brother Jim joined the Marines," Tom said.

Jim Seramba's old man was a foreman at the mine; Jim had dropped out of high school in his third year to go down the mine too. Switching services to the US Navy, he was assigned to the light cruiser *Juneau*, which was later sunk by the Japanese during the Battle of the Coral Sea, sending him, along with the five Sullivan brothers, down to Davy Jones' Locker.

The Greyhound bus headed east, following the twisting macadam highway amid cornfields and pastures now bleak with winter's bareness. The red barns were swelled with winter's silage, their outside walls plastered with advertisements, such as "Chew Red Man Tobacco." Monotonously repeated on small signboards stuck along the road was "Burma Shave" ... "Burma Shave" ... "Burma Shave." Looking at the frozen streams that hung from the hillside cuts, Tom's brain felt frozen, too, awaiting the flow of spring water when life would be revived.

The boredom weighed heavily on Tom, inducing sleep. The excitement of departure was over; he'd kissed his girl good-bye, but all he could now remember was the eternal question in the army: "Why am I waiting?" Nobody had an answer. Certainly nobody on that bus.

Tom rested his head against the vibrating window and closed his eyes, thinking, *I wish I could find a place where I could lie down in the deep grass and sleep for twenty years, like Rip Van Winkle, until this war is over. Nola and I would walk on the dusty roads of summer, over the wooden bridge. I'd carry my fishing pole over my shoulder, and we'd see June bugs darting on the pond, with darning needles poised in the air above the surface. We'd take our shoes and socks off and feel the mud between our toes. Trout would hide in the still pools at the stream's edge.*

*In the fall, horse chestnut trees would drop their spiny seeds, while inside the chestnut would be reddish brown and smooth to the touch. The osage orange would be soft and pulpy, and not an orange at all. The persimmon would taste bitter, and makes our lips pucker. Garter snakes would sun themselves on the rocks. If we disturbed them, they would slither away in the grass.*

The Greyhound bus was arching over the white fields, passing barns that pulsated in the white light.

Tom awakened with a start. *I hope this war ends soon, so I can go back home, go to college, and get a good job. Then I'll marry Nola, as I promised.*

# CHAPTER 8

· · · · · · · · · · · · · · · · · · · · · · · · · · · · · ·

In April PFC Tom Blaine finished basic training and got a three-day pass. The scuttlebutt was that Company C would be shipped immediately overseas to Europe. It was the first time in his life that Tom had been separated from his family for more than a few days, but now he was back in their bosom again, finding that his father's attitude toward him had changed. The old man marched him down to Grogh's Tavern to show him off in his army uniform, but John's pride was somewhat mitigated when his son drank only one beer. Sarah managed to come home from the WACs to see her middle brother before he was shipped overseas. The only fly in the ointment was that Jim was in Camp LeJeune. But young Luke made up for Jim's absence by continually asking Tom about the army.

Tom wanted especially to be with his fiancée, not having seen Nola for three months, but that was long enough for them to feel shy with each other at least at first. Nola tried, again unsuccessfully, to persuade her mother to come to dinner at the Blaine home, but her disappointment was assuaged by her future mother-in-law's sympathetic understanding of her situation. But Tom did not understand, despite having his mother's support.

Nola had come to recognize that Tom's mother was the protagonist of the Blaine children, having given them birth, nurtured them, reared them, and given them her moral values while expecting nothing in return. Tom feared that Nola might consider herself a cut above the Blaines, socially speaking, as her mother did. He had not considered that Nola, like his mother, had a will of her own.

For three days Tom had talked hourly with his fiancée, fearing that they'd failed to forge a bond between them. So despite their endless talk and Tom's countless professions of love, Nola had rejected all his entreaties that they get married immediately. On the last day they climbed the hill and watched the sun set over the Appalachians.

At Camp Dix, Tom's thoughts quickly turned inward, for the first night back he hardly slept at all, staring blankly into the darkness. Company C was still awaiting orders to be shipped overseas. As Tom lay awake, he wondered if Nola's mother would have upbraided her again about him.

☀ ☀ ☀

"What you see in Tom is beyond me," Grace Henze said to her daughter. "They have no social status in this town. The father is little more than the town drunk. Nola, believe me, I worry about you. You must reconsider your engagement!"

"Mother, why don't you understand that I'm in love with Tom?" Nola protested, desperate at her mother's refusal to accept Tom as her son-in-law—or to accept the Blaines, for that matter.

"Nola, it isn't love that you feel for Tom, it's infatuation,"

Grace insisted. "You're just too blind and too young to know the difference."

"Mother, I've no doubt whatever of my love for Tom. I've promised Tom that I'll marry him just as soon as he gets home from the war, and that's what I intend to do."

"You shouldn't have made him such a promise. What if Tom gets killed in the war? Where will you be then? You've no idea of the chances you're taking. I don't want you to be hurt, dear, but I can't imagine why you think he will be faithful to you. Once he gets to Europe, he won't resist temptation; he'll sleep with any woman he can. Boys are like that, you see. They can't resist temptation. You're being very foolish to make him such a promise."

"Mother, I've already done it, and it's a promise I won't back out on," Nola insisted.

"When you find yourself destitute, who'll support you?" Grace asked, as if she hadn't heard a word. "Please don't come to me for charity, because I'll tell you that you've made your own bed and you must lie in it."

"Please, Mother!" Nola wailed, pressing her hands to her ears.

"Your brother treated me abominably, running off to marry a floozy from Grogh's Tavern." Grace was close to tears. "Don't you see that Burt insulted me by marrying a cheap barmaid?"

"Mother, Burt and Lucy are happily married with two lovely children."

"Does that mean that I should be grateful?" Grace asked with biting sarcasm, as tears welled in her eyes. She began to speak in a softer tone. "Baby, please don't put your mother through this hell again. Don't you think that I've suffered enough? Nola, I beg of you, don't do this. Don't you think that Burt's shame was enough to last me a lifetime? You shall drive me to madness if you go on like this!"

Feeling badly shaken, Nola left her mother and went downstairs to speak with her father, who was glumly seated in the storeroom, having overheard the painful scene above.

"Daddy, what should I do?" Nola asked, looking into her father's sheepish face. "Mother wants me to reject Tom. Don't you like Tom?"

"Oh, Tom's all right," Fred said. "In fact, he's a very fine boy. But, Nola, you must make this decision for yourself. Do what you think is best for you. Of course your mother's upset—she usually is—but she'll get over it in time. Don't pay any attention to us, because we had it all out with Burt's marryin' Lucy, which your mother never accepted. The only difference is that you're a girl, and a girl wishes to get on with her mother. Burt didn't waste time askin' our permission, but a girl's different and doesn't wish to hurt her mother if she can help it, 'cause that's important to her. I can understand how you feel, but you must make up your own mind and forget about us old fogies."

"Daddy, I've decided that I won't marry Tom!" Nola wailed as tears filled her eyes. "I'll write him a letter and send him back his ring."

"There, there, Nola." Fred patted her back. "You don't have to send back the ring if you don't want to, as you've got the time. But if you've made up your mind, do what you think is best."

"Daddy, I have made up my mind!" Nola exclaimed. "I'll write and send him back the ring."

Nola ran upstairs and told her mother of her decision, but Grace had overheard everything. "Baby, believe me, it's for the best," Grace assured her daughter with an insipid smile as she held her close.

A day later, Tom opened Nola's letter at the base post office. The diamond ring fell out, bounced on the floor, and rolled beneath the desk provided for the convenience of customers. Tom fell to his knees and looked for the ring behind the wastepaper basket, while Dave Coulton wisecracked to his buddies, "What's happened to Tom? Did Nola send him the ring back? Why doesn't he stop looking for it and read her Dear John letter?"

The other inductees guffawed as if it were the funniest thing they'd ever heard—or seen, for that matter.

"Hey, Tom, when you find that ring, put it through your nose!" one inductee said.

"Hey, Tom, when you find it, put it on your dick!" another inductee advised.

Having found the ring, Tom stood up, red-faced, but he made no response to their taunts. He acted as if they weren't there. Maybe they weren't there, because he was there only in spirit.

After being on the firing line all morning, Tom was assigned to kitchen duty, and it was eight o'clock before he had a chance to write to Nola; the lights were turned out at nine.

*Camp Dix, N.J.*
*April 15, 1942, 8 p.m.*

*Dear Nola,*

*I got your letter this morning, in which you sent back my ring. Nola, I feel sick at heart, because I've always loved you. We've just gotten orders, so we'll be shipped out fast, maybe in a day or two, maybe sooner.*

*Nola, I can't put my feelings into words, but you're the only girl I've ever wanted and wished to marry. Now I'll have to forget about that! How can I forget about you when you're the only future I have, and now that isn't going to happen.*

*I know that your mother is against me, because she refused to come to my house to celebrate our engagement. That must have put a strain on you, but if your mother had come, she'd have seen how happy we are together because of our love for each other.*

*Nola, I can't believe that you've changed your mind. All that I ever wanted was that we should be happily married and have a family.*

*Nola, I still feel you in my heart, which is telling me all that you mean to me.*

*It's lights out! Nola, I'll finish this tomorrow.*

*4:30 a.m.*

*Nola,*

*I've just got a three-day pass, which starts tomorrow. I WILL PHONE YOU TODAY!*

*My dearest love,*
*Tom*

"May I speak to Nola?" Tom asked that morning, speaking from the pay phone at the PX.

"This is a collect call. Will you accept the charges?" the operator asked.

"Tom, is that you?" Fred asked.

"It's seventy-five cents for the first three minutes," the operator cut in.

"Fred, I've only got fifty cents," Tom said. "Will you pay the charges?"

"Yeah, sure, operator, I'll pay. Put him through."

"Thank you, may I speak with Nola?" Tom asked.

"Nola, Tom's on the phone, askin' to speak with you," Fred called upstairs.

"Tom?" Nola said, a minute later.

"Nola, listen to me." Tom spoke quickly. "I've got a three-day pass before I'm shipped overseas. Can you take the Greyhound bus, the same one that I took outside the post office, and get here by noon tomorrow?"

"Please, Tom, I told you that I can't!" Nola cried.

"Nola, I beg of you! Just as soon as you get here, we'll catch the bus to Atlantic City and get married on Friday afternoon and have

90

our honeymoon. You see, I must be back on the base by midnight on Sunday. Nola, it'll be fun if you'll come. Won't you?"

"Tom!" Nola wailed. And the line went dead.

Tom changed a dollar at the soda fountain and repeatedly called back, but the operator told him that the phone had evidently been left off the hook.

Between hope and despair under the ethereal blue sky of the Pine Barrens, Tom plodded on through his day. Late that afternoon, Company C was dismissed; some men went to New York and some to Philadelphia or to points in between to spend their three days with family or girlfriends. That night Tom slept alone in the deserted barracks. Or rather he didn't sleep, for his mind was filled with real or imagined apprehension, and in his state of mind, he couldn't tell the difference.

*Nola might at least have sent me a telegram to tell me that she wouldn't be coming,* Tom told himself in the pitch blackness of night. *That would have eased my mind instead of making me feel like a rabid dog that some policeman shoots to put out of its misery before it bites someone. Grace is a problem, but maybe it's Fred too.*

The futility of these thoughts was like a corrosive acid burning in Tom's consciousness.

*Maybe I'm asking too much of her. Maybe marryin' a jerk like me is too big a step for her to take. Maybe a girl doesn't want to stand up to her mother, who's probably heaping scorn and ridicule on my head right now, telling her daughter that she'd be a fool to marry a no-account like me, who doesn't even have enough ambition to get a better job than working in a grocery store.*

*"What right does Tom Blaine think he has to ask for the hand of my daughter in marriage?"* Tom imagined Grace saying, telling her daughter that he wasn't worth the grief.

*But maybe Nola didn't even bother to show my letter to her mother. Maybe she was too embarrassed to tell her that I'd asked her to elope with me and get married. Maybe I should just get used to the idea of having to live without Nola. Didn't Dave Coulton say that too? Maybe Nola thinks I'm a gold digger. But she wasn't angry with Dave, because she kissed him good-bye when we boarded the bus. And I saw him kiss her in the balcony of the Alhambra, but Nola was always kissing boys there!*

*Why can't I get used to the idea of living without Nola? The Appalachian Mountains are still standing, even though we're not going to get married. That will at least be some consolation, come to think of it. If I were now on the summit of the hill, I could look straight across the blue ranges of the Appalachians. Damn Nola!*

A mile from the main gate of Camp Dix, the state highway bisects the Pine Barrens with geometrical precision, with Cal's Esso Station on one side and the Good Eats Luncheonette on the other. That Friday, just before noon, Tom stood on the wooden steps of the Good Eats Luncheonette, awaiting the arrival of the bus with Nola, which was running late. He wore a light-brown tweed jacket and a pair of pants of a darker shade, which he'd bought at the PX. And he carried a suitcase that appeared to be made of a composite material.

The sun beat down from above, casting a harsh light on the pale-green pines and the dark-green laurels that grew beneath. Having grown up in a hardwood forest, Tom had found the Pine Barrens of New Jersey a surprise after what he had grown up with in Pennsylvania. Thirty million years ago, the Atlantic Ocean had broken against Pennsylvania, where the Delaware River now flows, but the sea had receded to create the flat Pine Barrens.

*If I fell asleep, like Rip Van Winkle for twenty years, would it be thirty million years from now?* Tom asked himself.

Still there was no bus.

Having eaten breakfast at five at the PX, Tom felt hungry, so he stepped into the Good Eats Luncheonette, sat on a counter stool, and ordered a hot dog and a Pepsi. When his order came, he squeezed ketchup and mustard on the hot dog and added a couple of spoonfuls of relish. He ate quickly and drank the Pepsi, burping. He paid the waitress, whose hair was orange—as was her face.

Tom grabbed his suitcase, went outside, and stepped into the middle of the road, looking as far as he could to the west. Still no bus, and it was already twenty past noon.

*Maybe there isn't going to be a bus. Or maybe they've changed the schedule.*

"The bus is late," the orange-haired counter lady informed him when he stepped back inside.

"How late will it be?"

"I dunno, but it's late," she said, wiping the counter with a gray dishcloth.

Tom saw another PFC wearing a soiled uniform that did no honor to the army and playing one of the two pinball machines. The young soldier was playing a blonde portrayed on the pinball machine, who wore a tight, low-cut dress. Printed words issued from her mouth, saying, "Do you wanna score, Buddy?"

The private kneed the pinball machine, attempting to raise his score, but it flashed "Tilt!"

"Shit!" the young soldier exclaimed in a Southern drawl while Tom set down his suitcase to watch. "Well, ain't that a pisser! That must be the third time. Whaddya think, soldier? What gives here anyways?" The PFC's eyes were deeply sunken in his hatchet face.

"I don't think anything about it," Tom said, grinning.

"Well, whatcha lookin' at me for, den?" the young private asked. "Ain't you got nothin' better to do?"

"I'm sorry, but I'm waitin' for the bus."

"Where you come from, soldier?"

"Pennsylvania."

"Ya got good hooch over there?"

"I don't drink."

"Call it a weakness, but I do. I come from down Georgia where we got the real good stuff. Damn good stuff. The best. It comes from the mountains. Name's Whitehorse, Josh. What's yours?"

"Tom Blaine." He grasped PFC Whitehorse's hand.

"D'ya wanna try to beat my score?" Whitehorse asked.

"No thanks, I'm waiting for the bus." Tom looked at the clock behind the counter.

"I'll see ya 'round, den," Whitehorse replied dismissively.

"I'll see you." Tom picked up his suitcase and heading for the front door.

It was 12:30. The bus was half an hour late.

*Maybe Nola didn't get on the bus,* Tom thought for the umpteenth time, hoping and praying that she'd step from the bus right into his arms. *If she doesn't come, what will happen to me shouldn't happen to a dog, for it will be kaput with me. That'll be the end of it. I can see it coming. Kaput, because I won't have any future. Not without Nola, I won't. It was only a lot of wishful thinking.*

Hoping against hope, Tom fervently prayed. That's how tense he'd become. His whole future was right before his eyes, and nothing else mattered. Why should it? He wouldn't have a future without Nola.

*Anyway, if Nola doesn't come, my future doesn't matter. But that's not going to happen, because I think she's coming. But how long do I have to hope and pray and wait? Hoping and praying and waiting, but for what?*

He looked down the long, straight, white highway in the stark sunlight. *Why are people so casual here? Can't they see by just looking at me that my whole future, everything I've ever hoped and dreamed for, is on the line? If Nola doesn't come, nothing is going to happen to me. Zilch!*

*Maybe I should forget about her, pretend she doesn't exist. Think only of yourself, Tom. I've got to pull myself together and stop thinking about Nola, for crissake! Anyway, if she didn't get on the bus, it's because her ol' lady wouldn't let her, telling her I wasn't worth knowing, for crissake. Tom's a jerk!*

"Hey, there's the bus!" Tom exclaimed as he stared down the long road that bisected the Pine Barrens with hardly anything on either side except pine trees and more pine trees that seemed to go on forever. The bus glinted in the sunlight as the whole world on either side revolved around it. It was just a silvery speck that grew larger and larger, finally stopping and emitting exhaust fumes as the sunlight glittered on the windows.

*I wonder if Nola's in there.* Tom looked at the bright windows, unable to see anything inside but believing Nola was inside. He rushed to the door and was confronted by the debusing passengers, each intent on buying a hot dog, a hamburger, a Coke, or a Pepsi at the Good Eats Luncheonette.

"Nola!" Tom cried, catching sight of her and rushing forward to put his arms around her and kiss her. "Nola, I thought you weren't coming!"

"Tom, I tried to phone you."

"Gawd!" Tom exclaimed as if his brain were going "Tilt!" like a pinball machine.

"Tom, I'm famished."

"We can eat right here at the luncheonette, while I buy the tickets for Atlantic City," Tom said, grabbing her suitcase and his own.

"Tom, shall we wait to get married?" Nola asked as they entered the luncheonette, her blue eyes fixed on his as they sat at the counter. "There's still time, you know, if you wish to change your mind?"

"Nola, I don't want to change my mind about you. I'm finished waiting! I didn't come this far to wait!"

"The Moon Motel's just down the road a piece," Whitehorse said, appearing between them.

"What's that?" Tom asked.

"Howdy do." Whitehorse greeted Nola with a grin.

"Nola, this is PFC Josh Whitehorse," Tom said.

"I'm pleased to meet you," Nola replied with a look of surprise.

"Nola, you order me a hot dog and a Pepsi while I go and buy the tickets to Atlantic City," Tom said.

"Tom, whatcha goin' to AC for when the Moon Motel's right down the road?" Whitehorse asked.

"We're goin' to get married," Tom said.

"Good luck to both of you—an' have a good time!" With that, Whitehorse returned to the pinball machine.

Before they'd gotten their order, the bus to Atlantic City was announced, so they boarded the bus, sitting in the next-to-last seat at the back while the other passengers sat up front. Tom took the window seat, and Nola rested her head against his shoulder, wondering why he was so harebrained and how she could ever make a husband of him.

"Nola, I've got my month's pay, sixty-two dollars," Tom said. "That'll be enough to pay for the hotel and our marriage license."

"Don't worry, Tom, because I've brought some money too," Nola said as she kissed his cheek.

Tom felt grown-up, more grown-up than he'd ever felt before, and he'd every right to feel that way with a month's pay burning a hole in his pocket and his fiancée beside him. For such a man the future is always bright. And so it was for Tom Blaine on the Greyhound bus on the highway that bisects the Pine Barrens with geometric precision on the way to Atlantic City.

# CHAPTER 9

· · · · · · · · · · · · · · · · · · · · · · · · · · · · · · ·

THEIR ROOM AT the Ocean View Hotel in Atlantic City belied its name, for it had but one window that looked out the back of the hotel. Though they would have enjoyed an expansive ocean view of the Atlantic Ocean, they wouldn't have seen it anyway. They were on the sixth and top floor of a hotel that might as well have been the Moon Motel, which would have been a lot cheaper. Really, it wasn't that expensive, and they didn't care that they couldn't see the Atlantic Ocean.

The Ocean View Hotel didn't advertise in the Sunday travel sections of the *Philadelphia Inquirer* and the *New York Times* unless you call a small ad at the bottom of the page advertising. It offered a three-night weekend stay, Friday to Sunday, with Friday thrown in gratis. The hotel depended largely on spillover traffic—people in the summer season who hadn't gotten into the more expensive hotels because they were fully booked.

Tom and Nola were young and in love, so it didn't matter to

them. That's the way it is when you're desperately in love. It doesn't matter that the mattress is thin and hard and crunchy, maybe stuffed with old newspapers, and the varnish is peeling off the dresser, and the mirror has a crack running diagonally from top left to bottom right. Who notices such things when they're desperately in love, and it's the first time? You're all psyched up and don't even notice that your face in the yellow-stained mirror looked as if you were suffering from jaundice. That room would have gotten on Grace's nerves; if she'd seen it, she probably would have had kittens.

For Tom and Nola, it was just a bedroom. Maybe Nola was pretending not to notice it. But if you notice such things, you're not really in love either, and it's probably not the first time. At least not the way you were the first time, because when you're young you live fast or you don't live at all. When you start worrying about hotel rooms you're probably middle-aged, so it doesn't matter what you think, because you've already got a burgeoning waistline and you live in a house in a suburban subdivision. Call yourself middle class like all Americans do, even if your father works in a coal mine or keeps a grocery store.

Middle age hadn't yet arrived for Nola and Tom. Perhaps it never would. Hitler and Tojo had yet to be defeated first before they'd earn the right to live with central heating, thermostatically controlled, and every house looking exactly like every other house with a barbecue in the backyard. Maybe Nola and Tom wouldn't get that far. Maybe they wouldn't sleep on a box-spring mattress and wake up in the morning to hear the radio playing the news, music, or the weather and traffic report, brewing coffee at the same time. That's what the magazines and Norman Vincent Peale had promised—all the creature comforts for the American people. The boys would return home heroes and be worthy of such things—the only caveat being that they had to return.

But maybe that dingy hotel in Atlantic City would be the end of Tom and Nola's dream. Maybe that's why they'd jumped the gun, arriving in Atlantic City to get married and finding that the marriage bureau in the City Hall had closed at five and wouldn't be reopening until nine on Monday morning. So Tom had paid the taxi driver a dollar and a quarter, not including the seventy-five-cent tip, to drive them to the Ocean View Hotel, where they checked in to an eight-dollar-a-night room. But the room didn't matter, because Tom was young with feelings of both vanity and inadequacy. Afterward he remembered only the ineffable joy that he would never feel again, no matter how long he might live, for nothing else mattered, no matter how successful he might become or important he thought he was. He had woken up with the girl sleeping beside him that he wanted for his wife.

Upon reaching the reception desk, Tom had felt nervous writing their names for the first time, "Mr. and Mrs. Thomas Blaine." But the fishy-eyed clerk didn't believe him, and Tom didn't like being deceitful, not having told many lies. Nola thought that Tom had given them away, but she knew that was the price she'd have to pay to be with him. Just as Tom had known that lying was the price he'd have to pay and gladly pay if he was going to sleep with the girl he loved and wished to marry, but couldn't.

"Nola, you just wait, and one day I'll take you to a much better hotel than this dump!" Tom protested, setting down their suitcases beside the bed.

"I know you will, Tom," Nola replied, a light shining in her blue eyes. "You're the only boy I've ever loved—ever truly loved!"

"Someday, Nola, I'm goin' to be a big thumpin' success," Tom said. "Just you wait! We'll live in a big house out in the country and have lots of kids. We won't remember where we started."

"Tom, I'm so happy right now, just that we can be together."

They went down to the big empty dining room of the hotel and had pot roast, mashed potatoes, and peas. Afterward they went straight up to their room, even though it was only nine o'clock. Nola went down the hall to the bathroom while Tom sat on the edge of the bed to await her return. When Nola reappeared, she told him where the bathroom was, and when he'd returned, she was already in bed, wearing her nightdress. Quickly Tom undressed and slipped into bed beside her, taking her in his arms.

※ ※ ※

The following morning when Nola opened her eyes, it was six o'clock, and a flat, white light was shining on the dresser mirror. She placed her cheek on Tom's chest, then lightly touched his face with her fingertips till he stirred. Immediately Tom took her slim body in his arms, her softness passing through him for the umpteenth time that night. But he couldn't remember how many times, having fallen asleep only to be awakened again so that he couldn't remember. He drifted off again.

"Tom, wake up!" Nola said.

"What time is it anyway?" Tom asked, sitting up naked in bed and seeing Nola seated before the dresser in a wooden chair and combing her hair.

"It's eight o'clock. Aren't you going to get up and get dressed?"

"Why should I when what I'm interested in seeing I can see right before my eyes?" Tom said, resting his back against the headboard and stretching and yawning.

Nola stuck her tongue out at him in the dresser mirror.

"Nola, last night was the first time I've ever been intimate with a girl," Tom said.

"Why do you confess it?" Nola asked without looking around.

"It's hard to explain."

"Please try."

"Well, you see, I've thought about it so much, but the real thing is very different."

"How different is it?"

"It's hard to explain, just different."

"How different?"

"Well, it's more like a surgical operation, if you know what I mean."

"I like that!" Nola exclaimed.

"Now I suppose I've offended you?"

"No, I'm not offended."

"Nola, I want to remember you as you are right now, combing your hair and looking like Aphrodite. Does that sound sentimental or like something from the movies?"

"No, it doesn't to me."

"I wish I'd brought my good suit to get married in."

"I brought it with me," Nola said

"You brought my suit? Where'd you get it?"

"Where do you think I got your suit?" she asked, a smile on her lips.

"Did you go to my parents?"

"Yes, I did."

"Did you tell them we're getting married?"

"Yes, I did, thinking it best."

"Nola, you're acting like my old woman already!" Tom exclaimed joyfully. "What did my parents say?"

"They wished us the best."

"What about your mother? Did she come round?"

"She will, Tom, I'm sure, when she gets to know you. We'll send them a telegram just as soon as we're married."

"I'm freezing!" Tom declared as he sprang from the bed and began dressing quickly.

Nola turned to the mirror and resumed brushing her hair.

"Nola, you'd better get dressed, because your beauty is drivin' me crazy!" Tom exclaimed, placing his hands on her shoulders and kissing the nape of her neck.

Silently Nola continued brushing her hair.

"Okay, don't listen to me!" Tom muttered, pulling his T-shirt over his head.

"Are you going somewhere?" Nola asked.

"Not without you, Nola," Tom said as he pulled his pants up his legs.

"Are we going for breakfast in the hotel?" Nola asked. "I believe it comes with the room."

"Yeah, it does, but I wouldn't recommend this dump for anybody on their honeymoon."

"Honeymoon?" Nola asked with a teasing smile.

"What's the matter, Nola?" Tom asked, surprised.

"Doesn't the wedding come before the honeymoon?" she asked, a light in her eyes.

"Yeah, it does," Tom said, sitting down on the edge of the bed to put on his socks and shoes. "But in our case, it didn't, 'cause we couldn't get a marriage license until Monday."

"What if we've changed our minds by that time?"

Tom gave her a blank expression, not crediting what he was hearing.

"Perhaps you'd prefer a trial wedding?" Nola suggested mischievously. "Do you want me on thirty-day approval, like a trial offer?"

"Nola, we ain't got thirty days!" Tom replied, his face still blank. "Are you being serious or just kiddin'?"

"No, I'm suggesting a trial marriage."

"Nola, I never knew I could love you so deeply!" Tom exclaimed suddenly, seeing through her as he stood up and put his arms around her and kissed her lips.

"Tom, there are a lot of things you don't know about me," Nola said as she rested her head against his chest above his heart.

"What's my heart saying to you?"

"It's telling me that I must hold you very tight and never let you go."

"Does it tell you how much I love you?"

"Yes, I think it does!"

"Nola, can I listen to your heartbeat?"

"I'm sure you'll find that it will say the same thing."

Tom pressed his ear against Nola's breasts.

"What does it tell you, Tom?"

"Your heart is beating just like mine, and it's telling me that you love me," Tom said as he looked closely into her blue eyes.

"Yes, Tom, I think you're right," Nola said just before they kissed.

The dining room of the Ocean View Hotel did have a panoramic view of the Atlantic Ocean. But that morning there were few diners present to enjoy it. An elderly woman with an ear trumpet, sitting close by, stared at them when they entered and never stopped looking till they left.

Farther off was a corpulent gentleman breakfasting with his wife and two adolescent children, a boy and a girl. This gentleman divided his attention between eating and reading the financial pages of the New York Times, while ignoring his wife, who looked faded and harassed. She constantly admonished the children, who bickered and had bad manners. The boy finally knocked over his glass of milk, so that the waiter had to soak it up with a towel before bringing him another. The gentleman was busy all the while reading the newspaper, paying no attention to his wife, who looked as if she were about to cry.

When the family left, Tom asked Nola, "Did you see the way

that man ignored his wife? He treated her as if she didn't exist or was a kid herself. Marriage for her must be a trap."

"I'll bet she picks up his clothes too," Nola said.

"I'd never treat my wife like that," Tom insisted.

"If you did, you wouldn't find me sitting there watching you read the newspaper!" Nola exclaimed, laughing.

"But maybe she's more interested in the kids than her husband."

"Can you blame her?"

"Nola, this isn't the sort of conversation you'd expect to have on a honeymoon."

"Be warned then." Nola laughed as the waiter brought their order.

After breakfast, the couple walked to a jewelry store on the boardwalk, where Nola bought a silver wedding band for herself and one for Tom.

"Nola, I can't let you buy yourself a wedding ring—let alone one for me!" Tom protested when they'd left the store.

"Tom, when you become a big shot, you can buy me the most expensive ring you want, and one for you as well," Nola said as she took hold of his arm.

"But Nola, I don't feel right about wearing a ring."

"If you don't wear one, I won't either."

"You can't get married without wearing a wedding ring from me," Tom said.

"Do you think I want girls looking at you, thinking you're single?"

"What girls?"

All morning they strolled the length of the boardwalk. Then they had hot dogs for lunch at the Steel Pier. In the afternoon they sat on the beach, gazing at the blue-green of the Atlantic Ocean. Tom was delighted by the bright spring sunshine and the taste of the salty breeze from off the sea. Combers rose from the depths of the sea, moving majestically toward the shore and breaking with reverberating crashes against the beach. People who sat on the beach to get the sunshine were wearing street clothes, for it was too chilly to swim.

Nola and Tom removed their shoes and socks and walked hand in hand along the surf line, dashing gleefully back and forth between the waves until Tom got the bottoms of his pants splashed and the hem of Nola's dress was wet. Tom took off his jacket and spread it out on the sand so they could lie on it and gaze up at the clouds, which were propelled seaward by a southwest breeze. After a few minutes, Tom pulled his T-shirt off and made a bundle of it, which he used as a pillow.

"Be careful, Tom, or you'll get sunburned!" Nola warned, her blue eyes sparkling in the bright sunlight.

"Nola, can you see the castle in the clouds up there?" Tom asked, as if he hadn't heard.

"You don't wish to get sunburned, do you?"

"Yeah, I think I do," Tom replied, turning to look into her eyes. "I'd like to crumble to dust so that no one would be able to find me, no matter how hard they tried. What would you say to that?"

"Where would you be, Tom?" Nola asked, gazing into his brown eyes.

"Maybe I'd have gone to all those places that Richard Halliburton visited, starting right here."

"I believe that I'm done to a turn," Nola observed. "And if you don't watch out, you'll get sunburned."

"Did you hear what I just said?" Tom asked, propping his head on his elbow and looking at her face.

"You said something about Richard Halliburton," Nola mused dreamily. "Tom, if we lie here like logs, we'll get burned. At least I will."

"Nola, didn't I ask you something?"

"What did you ask me?"

"Didn't I say that I'd like to visit those places that Richard Halliburton did?"

"What's that got to do with getting sunburned?"

"Nothing!"

"Are you just daydreaming then?"

"Yes, about castles in the air!" Tom exclaimed, falling back on the sand. "Can you see that puffy, white cloud up there, the one that's got turrets on top with a streak coming out the front that looks like a road leading to a drawbridge?"

"Can you imagine what my mother would say if I told her that I married a man who sees castles in the clouds?" Nola asked as she turned to him with a smile on her lips.

"What would she say?" Tom asked, frowning.

Nola laughed and said, "She'd tell me that I'd married a man who was a poor prospect for a husband."

"Why doesn't your mother like me?"

"I've told you she'd like you if she knew you better," Nola insisted. "All she knows is what I've told her."

"Why's she so negative about me then?"

"I suppose because you see castles in the air. And because she sees only what she chooses to see."

"Did she tell you not to marry me?"

"Yes, she did."

"Is that why you sent my ring back?"

"Yes, I thought it best, but then I changed my mind, realizing I'd made a mistake. So here I am!"

"What made you change your mind?"

"Divine inspiration, I suppose."

"Do you mean that you didn't know?" Tom asked, looking hurt.

"Does any girl ever know for sure?"

"So, you just decided to marry me because that was the right thing to do?"

"Yes, I did, but it's not too late for you to change your mind, if that's what you want to do?"

"Nola, how can you say that when you know how much I love you?"

"What about Richard Halliburton then?" Nola asked, smiling.

"What about him?"

"If you marry me, you won't be able to travel to all those romantic places. Won't that be a big disappointment to you?"

"No, it won't."

"Why do you say that?"

"I just told you why."

"Tell me again."

"Because I love you so much."

"What do you love most about me?"

"Not what you're thinking!"

"Tell me?"

"I love you because you always are yourself," he said, leaning over to kiss her lips.

"Till this moment, I don't believe that I ever knew you."

# CHAPTER 10

· · · · · · · · · · · · · · · · · · · · · · · · · · · · · · · · · · · ·

AT EIGHT-THIRTY MONDAY morning, Tom and Nola called at
Dr. Schofield's office in a three-story commercial and professional
building a block from City Hall, where they had their blood tests,
for which they each paid ten dollars. At nine they went to the
marriage license bureau in City Hall and then to another building
close by, where they were married before a justice of the peace, Mr.
John Stanziker.

"Lemme see if I can get you a couple of witnesses," the justice
of the peace told them before stepping into the corridor and calling,
"Belle, willya come here a moment—and where's Lew got to?"

"I just seen him," Belle replied.

"Go an' get him, willya?"

Belle interrupted her mopping to search for Lew, the janitor,
so that the justice of the peace could marry them according to the
law. When the brief ceremony was over, the newlyweds descended
in the elevator to the main floor.

"Well, Nola, what do you think St. Peter's going to say, since we've been living for three days in sin?" Tom asked as they stepped out into the bright sunlight and he took her hand.

"Actually, Tom, it was two days, to be precise," Nola said as they headed for the boardwalk.

Tom laughed. "Okay, but three nights, and I'm only countin' the nights!"

"You conceited male!" Nola exclaimed, laughing herself.

"Did you see the expression on the justice's face when I told him we'd jumped the gun?" Tom asked, grinning.

"Why did you have to tell him such a thing?"

"I guess I was feeling proud—and it just slipped out."

They strolled on the boardwalk hand in hand under a cloudless blue sky with a gentle southwest breeze blowing. In the summer, the southwest breeze pumped hot, humid air from the Gulf of Mexico, but in April it was delightful. The fine weather had brought visitors to Atlantic City, some of them strolling along the boardwalk while others were pushed in wicker cars by Negroes. And some were seated on the verandahs of the hotels.

Nola had the demure expression of a new bride, which was matched by her brown suit and white silk blouse.

"She's beautiful!" a white-haired gentleman announced to Tom, as he tipped his hat. "Son, I want you to take good care of her, hear me?"

"Indeed, sir, that is what I intend to do," Tom exclaimed, filled with pride. "We've only just got married."

"Congratulations to you both!" the older gent said, again lifting his hat.

"Thank you very much, sir!"

"Do you intend to tell everyone that we've just got married?" Nola asked.

"Nola, I can't not tell the whole world how happy we are," he replied, grinning. "You don't imagine that any of these old people are enjoying themselves as much as we are?"

"Certainly, not as much!" Nola conceded, smiling as she squeezed his hand.

"Most of the people are too old to have that much fun anyway."

"That depends on what you mean by *fun*?" Nola said with a mischievous gleam in her eyes.

Blushing, Tom said, "Nola, do you think I'll ever get tired of it?"

"Tired of what?"

Tom quickly did a double take.

"Tired of it or of me, do you mean?" Nola asked.

"Neither!" Tom exclaimed happily.

"So, you'll have to wait till you're old and gray to find out?"

"I'll never be that old!"

"Well, at the moment, I can't imagine either of us being that old," Nola confessed with a chuckle.

"Nola, when we're old and gray and doddery, we'll come back to Atlantic City to be pushed along the boardwalk by a Negro," Tom said. "We'll be wearing our best bib and tucker, looking like two old fogies and glad to have the sun shining on our withered faces. But still, Nola, it doesn't seem natural to me, because I can't get used to the idea of us being old."

"Don't talk about it then."

"Yeah, I sure hate to think like that," Tom said, a premonition passing through him. *Maybe this is the only time that Nola and I will be together.*

"Tom, I'm so happy just being with you!" Nola suddenly exclaimed as she leaned over to kiss his cheek.

"Nola, we're always goin' to be happy together, no matter what," Tom said confidently, putting his arms around her and kissing her lips.

"Tom, we'll always face life together, no matter what it brings," Nola reassured him as she stared into his brown eyes.

"Nola, why shouldn't I be happy when I've got the girl I love—my wife—in my arms? I've gotta ask myself, Can things get any better? And look, the sun's shining!"

"Then don't act as if you've got one foot in the grave and the other on a banana peel." Nola laughed as the idea struck her as absurd, for she was dispelling her worst fears.

"Huh?" Tom asked with a look of surprise.

"Tom, already in my mind I see that the war is over and that you've returned to me. If we could only jump ahead and forget everything and have the war ended."

"That's how I feel, Nola. When this war ends, I'll come home with an honorable discharge and go to college. After graduation I'll start making big bucks. Nola, just you wait! I'll become a great big thumping success! Once I've got an education, it won't be a question of knowing the right people or being at the right place at the right time. I'll be able to take care of myself, not waste my time working in a grocery store. I'll have big ideas about myself, Nola. Maybe I'll work for a big corporation and rise straight to the top. Nola, I hope you don't think I'm just bragging?"

"No, Tom, I want my husband to be ambitious," she said with a sweet smile. "I want my husband to be a good provider."

"Yeah, I will be, Nola," Tom reassured his young bride. "I'm going to make you proud of me. We'll have a big house way out in the country with plenty of rooms for our kids to sleep in, and we'll have a big garden. We'll buy one of those old farmhouses in the country. Twenty years will pass before we know it, because we'll be so happy we won't notice how happy we are. When our kids are grown, we'll come back to Atlantic City."

They sat on a bench with Tom's feet on the boardwalk rail, and they gazed at the ocean, where little waves—hardly waves at all—were lapping against the shore just like an affectionate dog that licks its master's hand.

*Maybe this isn't the first time, but the last time that I'll see the Atlantic Ocean.* The thought had come to Tom out of the blue. *Maybe it's a premonition of consciousness from the depths of my mind. Maybe it's fate or God. Or maybe it's just my own fears and forebodings before the unknown. Whatever it is, it's like a physical sensation, part of my consciousness. Maybe I should call it love, for like fate and Nola, it's all tied up and comes to the same thing.*

At that moment Tom felt like a juggler, keeping three balls aloft. Or as if he were at a pinball machine flashing "Tilt!" For Tom's fear lay behind appearances, watching and waiting while he stared at the green-blue Atlantic or gazed into the cerulean blue sky above or looked at the Pine Barrens, where the little rivers with Indian names like Metedeconk and Allamuchy meander through the bright sunlight as they have done for thirty million years.

That morning Nola phoned the store, reversing the charges, and told her father that they'd just gotten married. After hearing his congratulations, Nola asked him how her mother had taken the news.

"Badly," Fred said, sparing her the details.

When Nola hung up, Tom asked, "Will your mother ever give us her blessing?"

"She might at least have spoken to me!" Nola said, possessed by her own thoughts and close to tears.

"Remember, the only thing that matters is our love for each other," Tom said, putting his arms around her possessively. "All that we've got to do is to convince other people of how much we love each other. That shouldn't be such a big problem if they've got eyes to see and don't make a big deal of it to start with."

"Tom, I don't want them to make a big problem." She smiled bravely as she dried her eyes with her handkerchief.

That evening was the last evening of Tom and Nola's honeymoon, so they splurged, ordering a lobster dinner in the hotel dining room. Tom got a half a bottle of the house wine, for Nola had persuaded him that a full bottle was too much. Tom knew that when he got back to Camp Dix he'd be broke, but spending his last dime didn't bother him. His future was happening right now, so he was eager to spend what money he had, and damn the expense. After all, their future might never materialize.

After dinner they strolled along the boardwalk. A light breeze was still blowing out of the southwest. Here and there lighted bedroom windows punctuated the façades of the big hotels. They stopped and paid four bits for six baseballs, and Tom knocked over three tenpins, winning a kewpie doll for Nola. On the wheel of chance, Tom lost three times, so the kewpie doll ended up costing him more than he expected.

At nine o'clock they returned to the Ocean View Hotel, where they paused at the lobby newsstand. Nola bought a romance novel, and Tom paid a quarter for the *Pocket Book of English Verse*. In their room, Nola sat on the bed with her back against the headboard to read her novel, while Tom sat hunched over on the wooden chair, his elbows on his knees, reading his paperback.

"What poem are you reading?" Nola asked him after a few minutes.

"Blake's 'The Tiger,'" Tom said without looking up.

"Do you like to read poetry?" Nola asked, seeing that his bony wrists protruded from the sleeves of his jacket.

"Yeah, I do," Tom said, looking up at her.

"Will you read it to me?"

Aloud, Tom read "The Tiger":

Tiger, tiger, burning bright
In the forest of the night,
What immortal hand or eye
Could frame thy fearful symmetry?

In what distant deeps or skies
Burnt the fire of thine eyes?
On what wings dare he aspire?
What the hand dare seize the fire?

And what shoulder and what art
Could twist the sinew of thy heart?
And, when thy heart began to beat,
What dread hand and what dread feet?

What the hammer? what the chain?
In what furnace was thy brain?
What the anvil? What dread grasp
Dare its deadly terrors clasp?

When the stars threw down their spears,
And watered heaven with their tears,
Did he smile his work to see?
Did he who made the lamb make thee?

"I don't understand what it means," Nola said when he'd finished.

"Does it have to have meaning?" Tom asked, frowning.

"Of course it does!" Nola cried with a laugh. "It has to mean something."

"Maybe it means different things," Tom suggested, straightening up.

"Tell me what it means to you," Nola replied.

"Well, the poem is about a tiger that lives in the jungle. This tiger, being a nocturnal creature, has very sharp eyes so that it can see in the dark. Every night it likes to roam through the jungle, because it fears nothing."

"Tom, you can't just make up the meaning as you go along," Nola protested.

"Maybe what the poet's saying: the tiger is always a tiger 'cause that's how God made it. Doesn't it mean that the tiger's always true to itself and not something else?"

"Yes, and tigers, unlike boys, can't change their spots."

"Leopards have spots and tigers stripes," Tom said, grinning at her.

"Smarty pants!"

"I guess that's why women read romance novels," Tom said, snapping the book shut.

"Male egotist!" Nola exclaimed, sounding offended.

"Nola, I'm sorry. Maybe I don't understand the poem. But I do think that the tiger is a beautiful animal—like you."

"Flatterer!" Nola stuck out her tongue. "I'm certainly not a tiger!"

"You're a tigress."

"Thank you very much, smarty pants!" Nola exclaimed again, jumping up and hitting him over the head with a pillow.

"Nola, I said I'm sorry!"

"No, you're not!"

"Yes, I am!"

"Come here then," Nola said, as she held out her arms to him.

Tom sat on the bed beside her and put his arms around her, while she encircled his neck as their lips met and they sank to the bottom of the sea, where there are no words, no roads back, but only their truth together.

# CHAPTER 11

· · · · · · · · · · · · · · · · · · · · · · · · · · · · · · · · · ·

ON TUESDAY MORNING at eight, Tom and Nola boarded the Greyhound bus in Atlantic City to take them to that crossroads in the Pine Barrens where Cal's Esso Station and the Good Eats Luncheonette stand, about a mile from the main gate of Camp Dix. Tom wore his army uniform, reminding him that he was AWOL—as if he needed reminding. They'd sat in the next-to-last seat in the back of the bus, the same seat they'd occupied before. The other passengers, of which there were only eleven—thirteen, counting the newlyweds—sat up front. An elderly couple seated directly behind the driver was eager to chew his ear, but evidently the driver didn't mind, or maybe he even enjoyed their company.

"Nola, as soon as you get home, I want you to write me," Tom said. "I want to know that you're home safe and that everything's all right, especially with your mother. I hope your mom will understand and accept the fact that we're now married. Before I left home and enlisted in the army, my dad acknowledged the fact that I was now grown up and on my own. He had to recognize that, you see, 'cause I'd enlisted. But now my mom's probably upset with me for not goin' home to get married. Now I figure that the sooner I get through this, the sooner I'll get back home, which for sure is what I want to do."

"Tom, I don't want you to be worrying about me," Nola assured her young husband as she looked into his brown eyes. "You must remember who you are and what kind of family you come from. I believe you'll be true to yourself, but I don't want you jumping up and volunteering for any crazy thing. No matter how foolish it might be, don't, because that isn't your nature, Tom, and never was. I've known you since we were in kindergarten together. You've always been a good, respectful boy and not a cutup like Jim. Tom, you're not a hero and were never meant to be one. Remember that you'll be coming home to me just as soon as this war is over, because I love you and need you more than anything else in the world."

Nola's words scared Tom, not that she meant to, but her fear was written on his face.

"Nola, there's no use pretending that this war will go away by itself," Tom said. "There's no way I can get around it by moping or shilly-shallying or pretending it isn't here. The only thing I can do is to face up to it."

Tom realized that he might have to kill someone, or be killed, to get to the other side. But he was determined to do his duty just as he was equally determined not to get killed himself. Wasn't it always the other guy who got killed, and you read about him in the newspaper back home? So Tom had promised Nola that he'd come back because he wasn't going to be the other guy, not if he could help it.

"Nola, I'll do my darnedest to see this thing through, so that I can come home and be with you just like I've promised," Tom reassured her, resting his head on the seat with his eyes closed.

"Whatever happens, I'll return to you, you see?" Tom opened his eyes, turning to gaze into Nola's blue eyes.

At ten the passengers were debused at the crossroads. Tom and Nola entered the luncheonette and ordered a hot dog and a hamburger, a Coke, and a Pepsi, for Nola had to wait an hour for the bus. She had already bought her ticket, so as soon as they had lunch, they left the luncheonette, wishing to be alone.

They began walking down the dirt, oil-sealed road that led straight to the main gate of Camp Dix, both feeling they could walk along that road forever just to be together, smelling the sweet-scented pines. But before they'd gone very far, Tom put his arm around her waist, guiding her into the springy pine needles beneath the pine trees. There they stood, holding hands, their eyes locked on each other as if they were staring into eternity.

"Nola, I should say something important now, but I can't think of a single thing to say that I haven't already said a thousand times. What I want you to know is that there's a force that works for good in the world, which we can find and believe in. I'm not going to worry about 'us' anymore, 'cause I know that you love me just as much as I love you and will be waiting for me no matter what happens. I know that as soon as I get back, we'll have our whole future to look forward to together."

"Tom, I want you to know that I love you more than I love myself, and I'll be waiting for you."

He exclaimed with rueful laugh, "Sometimes there are no words to say, and I'm the one who always believed in words. At school, the kids always kidded me, calling me the Walking Dictionary 'cause words meant so much to me."

Tears welled in her eyes as she said, "For almost four days we've been as one, and now we must part. Soon the only words I'll have from you will be written on paper or sent by mental telepathy."

At that moment, Nola's words seemed absurd to Tom, an

impossibility, for he'd held her close as a heartbeat for almost four days, never having been so close to anyone in his life before, except the mother who bore him.

After their last kiss and embrace, they set off back down the dirt road to the luncheonette, where they again quickly embraced and kissed for the last time, for the Greyhound bus had arrived. Nola boarded the bus, taking the next-to-last seat while Tom stood on the macadam highway and looked up to see her tear-stained face through the window, which her breath had misted. As the bus moved off rapidly, Tom ran beside it, but soon the bus was but the glint of a speck far down the straight highway, suspended between the Pine Barrens and the pale, clear blue sky.

Tom started down the dirt road, pausing once to straighten his tie and polish the tips of his brown shoes, rubbing them against his khaki pants. When he reached the main gate, he stood at rigid attention, saluting the MP. "PFC Blaine returning to base, sir!"

"Lemme see your pass, PFC Blaine," the MP ordered after returning Tom's salute. "Soldier, you're AWOL! Report immediately to Colonel Bricker."

"Yes, sir!" Tom responded as he saluted and took back his pass. He walked in a daze back to the barracks.

"Tom, where've you been?" was PFC Dave Coulton's greeting. "The colonel's going to ream your ass!"

"Nola and I just got married," Tom said, grinning sheepishly.

"Tom, you ain't just shittin' me?" Dave asked, looking surprised.

"Dave, why should I lie to you about that?" Tom asked, still grinning.

"Nola used to call you Goofball or Twinkle Toes!" Dave exclaimed, still unable to take it in.

"Dave, we're in love with each other," Tom said. "What's Colonel Bricker like?"

"He's regular army, an asshole, strictly follows regulations,"

Dave said. "Tom, he's goin' to throw the book at you 'cause he knows it backward and forward—and sideways too. Doncha know that goin' AWOL's serious?"

Tom shrugged, trying to make light of it, but he was scared. He knew that Dave was right. He'd seen Colonel Bricker strutting his stuff at the battalion review.

"Tom, Colonel Bricker's a Southerner, as dumb as they come," Dave said. "After the last war, the bastard stayed put in the army, 'cause he enjoys killin' so much, and he couldn't find a civvie job that would make him feel so self-important."

"What will Colonel Bricker give me?" Tom asked, looking frightened as a rabbit.

"The same he always does, six-and-six," Dave said.

"What's that?"

"Six months in the brig and six months' revocation of pay."

"But Dave, he can't do that. I've got a wife to support."

"You shoulda thought of that before you went AWOL."

Tom entered the barracks and ran straight into 1st Lt. Valens, who greeted him with "PFC Blaine, where the hell have you been?"

"Sir, I just got married."

"Congratulations!"

"PFC Coulton told me we're moving out to the firing range, sir," Tom asked hopefully.

"Soldier, you ain't goin' nowhere!" 1st Lt. Valens shouted in Tom's face. "Git yer ass over to Colonel Bricker, soldier!"

"Yes, sir!"

In the noonday sun, Tom approached the white bungalow, which was set off from the barracks by a canopy of pine trees. Stepping into Colonel Bricker's office, Tom was confronted by the diminished daylight, where he saw 1st Sgt. Murphy, Colonel Bricker's adjutant, in an outer office, guarding the colonel's door from unwanted intrusion.

"PFC Blaine reporting to Colonel Bricker, as requested, sir!" Tom said, saluting as he stood at rigid attention two paces before 1st Sgt. Murphy's desk.

"Soldier, you were ordered to report!" 1st Sgt. Murphy barked without looking up but returning a sloppy salute.

Standing for what seemed an eternity, Tom watched while 1st Sgt. Murphy shuffled papers, realizing that the sergeant was going to prove to him how unimportant he was. Maybe it was only for a couple of minutes, but to Tom it seemed an hour, for all he heard was the silence, which seemed to muffle his ears as the sweat trickled down his sides. Finally 1st Sgt. Murphy pulled himself to his feet and stepped to the partially opened door, where his head disappeared so that he looked like Brom Bones, the headless horseman. A brief, staccato exchange took place—*ra-ta-ta-tah*, like the sound of machine-gun fire—after which the horseman's head reappeared, his eyes expressionless like those of a dead fish on a bed of ice. He jerked his head and barked, "Colonel Bricker will see you now, PFC Blaine!"

"Thank you, sir!" Tom exclaimed, scared shitless as he stepped forward, sidling past 1st Sgt. Murphy's pendulous belly, which half blocked the doorway.

Tom stepped to within two paces of Colonel Bricker's desk, where he stopped, stood at rigid attention, saluted, and announced, "Sir, PFC Blaine reporting to Colonel Bricker as ordered!"

Colonel Bricker looked up and fixed his gray eyes on Tom with an expression of mild surprise. "At ease, PFC Blaine," he ordered, saluting and rising to turn to the window behind his desk where there was nothing to see except more pine trees.

Tom had a momentary vision of Colonel Bricker's elongated face with tawny skin that was the color of kid leather. Tom had moved his left foot a comfortable distance from his right, as he'd been instructed. He waited for Colonel Bricker to speak.

"Well, soldier, I've been listenin' ta hear what you've got to say," the colonel began with a soft Southern drawl that seemed to Tom to be saying, "Yeah, I've heard it all many times before. There ain't nothin' that's goin' to surprise me."

Colonel Bricker spoke to him with fatherly solicitude, saying, "Don't worry, son, everything's goin' to be all right. You see, I happen to be God, but I can be a God of vengeance or of kindness. Do you know the difference, son?"

"Tilt!" Tom's brain said to him.

"Soldier, you were absent from this base without permission, weren't you?" Colonel Bricker intoned as he gazed out the window.

"Yes, sir, I was!"

"Why was that, soldier?"

"Because I got married, sir!"

Upon hearing this, Colonel Bricker slowly turned around and fixed his gray eyes on PFC Blaine. "Soldier, did you just tell me that you got married?" the colonel asked as a smile lit his face.

"Yes, sir, I did!"

"Well, I expect now you want me to congratulate you?" Colonel Bricker asked with a sardonic grin of amusement, or contempt. "Is that why you went AWOL?"

"Yes, sir, it was!"

"'Cause you wanted to get married?"

"Yes, sir, I did!"

"So you didn't have time to think about anything except getting married?"

"Yes, sir, I didn't!"

"Soldier, how old are you?"

"Eighteen, sir!"

"Were you drafted, soldier?"

"I enlisted, sir!"

"Didya now?"

"Yes, sir, I did, along with a lot of guys from where I come from."

"Where's that, soldier?"

"Ridgeton, Pennsylvania, sir. It's a small town in the anthracite coal mining region, sir."

"Soldier, do you mean to tell me that you couldn't get married and get back to this base by lights out on Sunday, like everyone else?"

"Sir, the marriage license bureau didn't open till nine on Monday morning."

"Soldier, in a couple of days your unit will be shipped overseas. Do you wanna go with them?"

"Yes, I do, sir!"

"Well, soldier, I'll give you your wish," Colonel Bricker said. "I'm goin' to overlook your havin' gone AWOL. Pretend that it didn't happen. Soldier, will my confidence in you be misplaced?"

"No, sir!"

"Maybe you thought that by going AWOL you could stay behind. Was that your game, soldier?"

"No, sir, it wasn't!"

"Soldier, it's good to see that human nature hasn't changed that much," Colonel Bricker concluded with a benign smile. "In the Great War—that's what we called it back then, before this one came along—we were as gung ho to kill the Krauts as you are. So things haven't changed that much. The boys today have the same *esprit de corps* that we had, despite those intellectuals, pacifists, and pinkos who say this generation won't fight, 'cause there's nothin' worth fightin' for. We've become too civilized to be patriotic, thinking that we were too dumb to know the difference. But now you're tellin' me that this isn't so for this present generation, 'cause you're just as determined as we were. Soldier, that's why we need the infantry, the Queen of Battle, after all. Is that what you're tellin' me, soldier? Or am I just whistlin' Dixie? Soldier, what did you say your name was?"

"PFC Blaine, sir."

"That's a common enough name, soldier," Colonel Bricker observed, fixing his sad, gray eyes on Tom as they flickered like marsh gas. "Soldier, someday I want to have a long chat with you, but now ain't the time. I'll invite you down to Louisiana, and you can bring your wife and kids. I'll take you fishin' on the bayou and say some things to you when the time is ripe. Never mind about that now. I never had a son, but only a couple daughters. Remember, soldier, you'll be comin' down to visit me."

"Thank you, sir, I will!"

"Now get the hell outta here, soldier, and lemme see if I can straighten out this mess you've made."

"Thank you, sir!" Tom said, turning to go.

"Soldier!"

Tom stopped and turned around.

"Soldier, do I look like a coat rack?"

"No, sir!" Tom exclaimed, quickly saluting.

When Tom got back to barracks, Company C was moving out to the obstacle course, having just returned from the firing range. He fell into line with his platoon, knowing that he'd have to crawl on his stomach beneath barbed wire, carrying an M-1 rifle and a full field pack, with bullets whizzing a few inches above his head.

*Maybe I should have asked Colonel Bricker what's the purpose of this exercise. I'm sure there must be some reason for everything they do in the army, even the obstacle course. Maybe it's to instill* esprit de corps. *But if* esprit de corps *is so important, why do they use French, when hardly anybody knows what it means? Colonel Bricker would probably tell me that everything in the army is done according to regulations, and fuck the individual, 'cause there ain't no individuals in the army; that joker got himself killed last week.*

The next weekend was Tom's last before being shipped overseas. He didn't get a pass and didn't even bother to ask for one, knowing he wouldn't get one because he'd gone AWOL. During his last weekend in the empty barracks, his thoughts turned inward, for he was thinking of what he had to face when he got overseas. Whatever it might be, there was nothing he could do about it, because it was there, waiting for him to come. That evening he sat on his bunk in the empty barracks, wanting to write to Nola, but he needed to read a letter from his mother first.

*April 17, 1942*

*My Dear Son,*

*Nola brought your good suit and showed me her wedding ring, saying she'd paid for it and yours too.*

*Tom, I do hope that you know what you're doing, because you've got your father at a total loss. We both think that you should have waited to get married at home, which would have been the right thing to do. Now what am I going to tell the Reverend Stoppelmoor?*

*All that your father and I ever wanted was that you get a good education, so that you might find a good paying job. Send home your army pay, and I'll put it in the bank, where you already have a hundred dollars, including the interest. Your good suit I'll have dry-cleaned and put in mothballs for when you come home. Luke wanted your room, so he carried your books and rocks up into the attic.*

*Think about yourself, Tom, what you want out of your life. Nola's to become an army nurse, which I think you probably know. Sarah comes home some weekends, and Dan's training for the US Army Air Force in Georgia. Jim's still in California training for the Marines, but expects soon to be shipped somewhere in the Pacific.*

*I've just finished a biography of the life of Anne Boleyn and would gladly chop King Henry the Eighth's head off for his attitude toward women.*

*Dad's been reading the newspaper and says, "Hi! Do you need any money?" That's a big change for him!*

*With love,*
*Mother*

# CHAPTER 12

• • • • • • • • • • • • • • • • • • • • • • • • • • • • • • •

IN THE GRAY early-morning light, the USS *Belleau Wood* slipped past the jagged skyline of Lower Manhattan. Tom had never seen New York City before. *It looks to be a better place than I've ever seen. Infinitely better, only, as they say, you can't get there from here. I wonder if New York is just made up of a lot of people trying to make money. Riding subways or shooting up in elevators of skyscrapers—maybe these people are too busy making money to even bother to notice the city.*

Passing between the Narrows, the *Belleau Wood* entered the Lower Bay to be greeted by the Statue of Liberty, with her arm raised above the harbor. Turning eastward, the troopship began to rise and fall as it encountered the first deep-sea swells. Tom went below for breakfast, then stretched out on his bunk, the top of six stacked one on top of the other from floor to ceiling. He pulled a letter from Jim out of his fatigues' pocket and saw that it had the Marine Corps insignia at the top. He began to read:

*Oakland, California*
*April 22, 1942*

*Dear Dogface,*

*Tom, when you read this I'll be heading overseas. I've just finished combat training with machine guns and mortars, so the Devil Dogs are ready for the Japs.*

*My purpose in writing is not to ask you about the US Army, but to congratulate you on getting hitched to Nola Henze, who's a swell gal with beauty and brains, for I just got your postcard from Atlantic City. Her old man's moola doesn't hurt much either!*

*Last weekend I went with a buddy to San Francisco and got to thinking of the time I took you to the cathouse in Wilkes-Barre to lose your virginity, but you stayed in the parlor downstairs, chatting with the tarts and reading them Walt Whitman.*

*This buddy of mine knows two hot tamales, Blanche and Vicky, who share an apartment in S.F. Larry took Vicky, while I succumbed to the charms of Blanche, alias Betty Grable! If you're ever in S.F., I'll give you their address without having to clear it with Larry. We've had enough films on sex already, the last a horror.*

*Mom's expecting you home before you're shipped out.*

*Well, I guess that's about it, Shitbird!*

*Remember to shoot the Kraut before he shoots you!*

*I love you, kid,*
*Jim*

Monotonous days followed monotonous days, the sun rising above the flat horizon in the east, then traversing the sky before sinking beneath the flat horizon to the west. Each morning Tom was wrenched to consciousness out of a dream. It always the same dream: he was with Nola on the summit of the hill above Ridgeton, gazing into her sparkling blue eyes in the sunlight. She was the center of his universe, all that he wished for and desired.

Day after day the troopship rocked gently in a moderate swell, like a baby being rocked in its cradle. Ever eastward the *Belleau Wood* steamed at fourteen knots per hour, from one flat horizon to the next, but never seemed to arrive. Low-silhouetted destroyers shepherded them, constantly sounding the sea, searching for submarines that might lurk beneath the surface, threatening death and destruction.

Morning and evening, it was always the same. Tom would stand forward, watching the bow split the sea asunder, with a white wake hissing from the sea. In the evenings he would watch the phosphorescent wake of the stern as the stars came out, wishing that he could run back on light feet to the girl he loved in Ridgeton.

*Be still, my heart, be still,* Nola would say to him as if she'd heard his voice in the gathering dusk, allaying his fears and telling him that all would be well. They would walk again on the quiet roads of summer with all their fears forgotten. Already he could hear the patter of little feet, the touch of a little hand, as he gazed into the blankness of the sea as the sun dimmed in the west, igniting the pale dome of heaven ever so slowly, and faded.

"Nola, tonight I wish I was Rip Van Winkle," Tom said aloud into the growing darkness. "I want to go to sleep and wake up twenty years from now, so that the war is over. That's how I feel tonight."

The sky was completely black with stars shining as eight hundred young men sailed ever eastward, Tom among them. They'd been taken from the scattered mining communities of the forest-clad Appalachians, where the dairy farms have red, humpback barns. The prow of the *Belleau Wood* was like a keen knife, splitting the sea, transporting its cargo of young men forever eastward.

*I wonder where we are now.* Tom asked himself. *Maybe we'll* reach England soon—with her castles and palaces, her knights and fair ladies. Or maybe it'll be North Africa, as the scuttlebutt says.

In his mind's eye, Tom already saw the ominous, deserted shore with low brown hills beyond. Already his backpack was wrenching his shoulder blades as he and his buddies clambered down the netting that covered the steel hull of the *Belleau Wood*.

*When I get to the bottom, how do I reach the landing craft?* Tom asked himself. *Do I just drop?*

Already the sea was erupted by geysers, like exotic blooms.

*If a bullet has my name written on it, will death come swiftly? Will it come out of the blinding sky with a clear flash?*

Tom saw the sun's rays beating down on the sea. He longed for the quiet days of home, and he whistled to himself in the darkness to allay his fears.

*How many more days before we get there? When all I want is to run back on light feet across the sea to Nola. My first words to her will be, "Nola, let's climb the hill tonight."*

But Fate answered, *No, Tom, you can't go back. You're already as good as dead. You might say that you died long ago. You see, no one has a claim on life. You'll be forgotten, just as if you never existed. So it's best not to think about the future, your wife and children, and quiet summer days.*

"Hey, Tom, that you?"

"Yeah, Dave."

"First Lieutenant Valens wants to speak to Company C, pronto!"

"I'm comin', Dave."

"Whatsa matter? You seasick? You got the heebie-jeebees?"

"Dave, it's this sailin' and goin' nowhere and waitin' for somethin' to happen," Tom confessed. "It's gettin' on my nerves."

"Doncha know that everybody feels the same?" Dave said.

"You've just gotta forget all about it, think of somethin' else— maybe Nola. Did you write her a letter?"

"Yeah, I just did."

"I expect that made it worse. I mean that you just got married an' all before we sailed?"

"Yeah, it did make it worse," Tom confessed.

When Valens entered, Company C dropped from the bunks.

"At ease!" Valens said.

Company C swayed drunkenly with the troopship, which reminded Tom of Ray Dowling Sr., who used to stagger home down Main Street from Grogh's Tavern every Saturday night, reeling from telephone pole to telephone pole.

"Soldiers, bright and early tomorrow morning we're arrivin' off the coast of North Africa at a place called Casablanca," Valens announced, sounding as if he had it all down pat. A Greek-American, Valens had gotten his name changed by US Customs at Ellis Island. He was muscular, and his eyes were too close together—or maybe he looked that way because his eyebrows almost touched. He had been raised in an Irish neighborhood of Chicago, which accounted for his brogue.

"Right now, the weather on the landing beaches looks okay, so the first thing tomorrow mornin', you're goin' to get your chance to show what good soldiers you are," Valens said. "Right now, we're sittin' ducks for any German sub operating from the Bay of Biscay down to the coast of North Africa. They're probably hightailin' it down here right now to see if they can knock us off. But they can't, because we're goin' to beat the Krauts at their own game. So, men, this is it! At oh-five-hundred hours tomorrow mornin', we're goin' ashore, and we're stayin' ashore to show those Krauts what stuff we're made of. Any questions?"

For a long moment, there was absolute silence. Then PFC Jarrold, who hailed from Toledo, Ohio, piped up. "First Lieutenant

Valens—sir!—will the US Navy take us up to the beach, or will we have to swim? Sir, you see, I never learned to swim."

Amid tension-relieving laughter, Valens replied as impassive as the bust of Caesar, "For your information, PFC Jarrold, the US Navy will drop us right on the beach. Then they'll be skedaddlin', 'cause as far as they're concerned, we're a one-way operation. So the US Navy will be gettin' outta there as fast as they can. Any other questions?"

Silence.

"Okay, soldiers, in twelve hours—less!—I want good reason to be damned proud of you—and good luck!"

Tom wrote to Nola, trying to sound cheerful and optimistic though he felt fearful and apprehensive. He wondered if she'd be able to read between the lines. Then he wrote to his parents, trying again to sound upbeat. He put the letters in the mail sack and quickly undressed, climbed into his bunk at the top, and pulled the blanket over his face. Until lights out at nine o'clock, he stared into the semidarkness, asking, *What if that's the last letter Nola gets from me? What will she think of my cheerful, optimistic attitude if I'm dead? Will she think I sound like a loony bird or that I'm just too ignorant, too stupid, to know the difference?*

After lights-out, Tom dropped from his bunk and sat on his backpack to write again to Nola by the weak light of a low-wattage bulb.

May 7, 1942

My Dearest Nola,

I just wrote you a letter, but am writing again because it wasn't enough if I don't come back to you. The brief time that we were together was the happiest of my life. If I close my eyes, we are still together, and I am kissing your sweet lips. My only wish is that I could say everything that I feel in my heart when we are together. I had hoped to get a letter from you before sailing, but maybe it will be at Casablanca, where we land tomorrow morning. Have you received any of my letters? I hope they're not at the dead-letter office at the post office. Why do they hold back letters?

Jim wrote from Frisco before sailing overseas. The same Jim, believe me!

Last night I dreamed about you climbing the hill that Sunday afternoon, and me being a dumb bunny not figuring out why you'd come, thinking that you couldn't be interested in me. Nola, that was the beginning for us, just as I hope that this is not the end. Puff! Now I'm just smoke! I sure hope not.

I see your beautiful face sparkling in the sea, and I know that we will always be the same. But, Nola, if something does happen to me, I want you to be strong, because I know that's how you are. You will always be in my heart.

Your loving husband,
Tom

# EPILOGUE

• • • • • • • • • • • • • • • • • • • • • • • • • • • • • •

THE SUN SPRANG from the low, brown hills, glittering on the sparkling sea. Attack aircraft filled the sky, their staccato fire reverberating in Tom's chest, as Company C clambered down the netted hull of the *Belleau Wood* to the landing craft. His shoulders were wrenched back by the heavy backpack, and the canteen bobbed on his hip. Passing over portholes that pierced the steel hull with geometric precision, Tom momentarily stared into one, seeing nothing before descending to the next porthole, where he saw a gob frozen like the frame from a motion picture, seated at a table, his legs up, taking a drag.

*Maybe he's nervous,* Tom thought. *Or he's eager to get underway as soon as possible—like 1st Lt. Valens said, to drop us grunts and hightail it outta here.*

"The guy's smokin'!" Tom shouted at the top of his lungs into the steel hull, which was punctured with rivets. "The guy's smokin'!"

When he reached the bottom of the netting, Tom dropped and became momentarily unconscious. He found himself lying on his back, staring up at the steel hull of the *Belleau Wood*. He could feel the motion of the landing craft beneath him. His backpack had broken his fall. So Tom pulled himself to his knees, feeling the chug of the engine as they moved away from the troopship. Standing up, he grasped the side of the landing craft and looked up into a cloudless blue sky filled with other landing craft that looked like June bugs forming a necklace as they bobbed and surged, each heavy with its human cargo. Slowly the necklace began to form a single strand that pointed at the beach, along with other strands.

*Nola, I just got your letter,* Tom said to himself as if she were there. *I'll read it tonight, when all this is over and done with. I'll read every word twice, maybe three times, maybe a thousand times till every word rises from the page, and I can see your beautiful face shining before me like it used to do. That at least will be some consolation, but I'll keep your letter till tonight before I read it, when it's quiet so we can climb the hill together just like we used to do.*

Tom touched the letter in the breast pocket of his jacket, above his heart. But the smell of the exhaust made him sick, so he puked, thinking that Jim was right. *I'm a coward! All I want to do is go back to Ridgeton, Pennsylvania, a small mining town in the Appalachian Mountains of eastern Pennsylvania. That's where I was born and went to school. I got my first job at Henze's Grocery Store, where I first worked after school and all day on Saturday. That's how I got to know Nola, although I'd known her from kindergarten. My eldest brother, Jim, is a US Marine, and my kid brother, Luke, is sixteen and still in high school. My sister, Sarah, comes between Jim and me, and she's joined the WACs. As soon as the war is over, she'll marry her sweetheart, Dan Willoughby, whose father is the branch manager of the Wilkes-Barre Bank and Trust Company in Ridgeton. Dan's now in the US Army Air Force.*

A muscle twitched in Tom's stomach, and he felt hot.

*I'm going to get through this somehow,* Tom reassured himself. *Get through it and forget about it! I remember hearing the tick-tock of the clock when I woke up in Dr. Burdock's surgery after Pop had knocked me out cold. Pop must have been very angry with me because of something I'd said. What did I say? I can't remember what it was. I woke up listening to the clock going tick-tock.*

Before Tom's throbbing eyes, the shoreline looked closer.

*I want to lie down in the green forest and smell the pine needles like I did in the Pine Barrens.*

Suddenly the third gray landing craft erupted into a geyser, followed by silence as time stopped. Scattered debris floated on the surface of the sea as unseen men drifted to eternity. Each was unconcerned as they headed toward the beach, which was now clearly visible. There were posts strung with barbed wire near the surf; some of the wires were broken, flapping uselessly. Further back, a low escarpment with brown hills beyond was illuminated by the barren sunlight, where unseen scorpions waited in the machine gun nests, peering out, ready to sting.

*Soon the sun will rise over the Appalachians. I wish I could be there now. I wish I were with Nola and that we could climb the hill to watch the sunrise together.*

Suddenly the landing craft grated against the beach, throwing them down. Tom quickly pulled himself to his feet and looked up as a flight of screaming Eagles shattered the air, strafing the beach with their low-flying precision against the brown hills, their staccato bursts reverberating in his chest.

The prow dropped open, and the sea rushed in, leaving Tom chest-high in water, holding aloft his M-1 rifle and pumping with his legs, as if he were a fetus being ejected from the womb, feeling neither the heat nor the cold. He ran onto the beach and fell flat on his face, tripped by ankle-high wire. Bullets whizzed above his head, just as they had done in the obstacle course at Camp Dix.

*In the eaves of barns, wasps will build their paper nests. My mother told me that she saw Halley's Comet in 1910, and that it will come again in 1985, when Nola and I will be two old fogies.*

Turning, Tom saw another plume in the sea and floating debris.

*This is the Atlantic Ocean that I saw at Atlantic City, where Nola and I had our honeymoon. I remember that one day the ocean was so calm you could hardly see the wavelets.*

The beach was the scene of staccato machine-gun fire, voices shouting, figures running, stumbling. Some were getting up and running again, while others lay still. Tom got up and ran farther up the beach, only to be tripped again by an ankle-high strand of wire. Figures around him slumped in death.

"Tom!"

"Dave!"

"That machine-gun nest up there is playin' hell with us! We gotta put him out!"

"Okay, Dave!"

"Keep your head down, fer crissake!" PFC Coulton bellowed, his eyes beneath his helmet looking like those of a ferret. "Mark's hightailin' it up on the left, and I'll be on the right. You cover us, and either Mark or I will drop a pineapple down his hole while you cover us."

Tom stared at the machine-gun nest in the dry, low-lying escarpment above the beach. Taking aim, he heard his father's voice telling him how scared he had been in the last war, as Tom was now. *But somehow Dad had gotten through, came out the other side, just like Mom always said.*

Slowly, deliberately, as his father had told him, Tom raised his rifle, took aim, and fired repeatedly into the black hole, from which glinted a shining barrel.

Suddenly there was a flickering light, followed by a sharp gnawing of teeth. And Tom could not feel his leg, could not feel it at all. An overwhelming darkness appeared before his eyes, fluttering like a blackbird.

*I'll read Nola's letter tonight,* he thought.

With dimming eyes, Tom saw the figures moving forward, but he could not see them advance, for there was a pounding in his brain that he could not bear.

*They'll be victorious,* Tom thought as he turned onto his back and tried to stare into the blue sky as a flight of Eagles split the air, spitting rain.

*Tom, another day you'll be with Nola, and you'll never part.* He knew it was God speaking.

Tom thought, *Then maybe we'll board the bus to Atlantic City to get married and have our honeymoon—but not necessarily in that order. We'll even have the same bedroom, which we won't bother to notice, because we'll be eager to get into bed. Nola, I just got your letter, which I'm keeping to read tonight. Are you sleeping now? When you wake up, you must climb the hill, when the dew is wet on the grass, remembering how happy we always were there together. Please come, darling. I'm waiting for you.*

Nola awoke with a sudden start. *Tom, where are you? I just felt you move beside me. But I must have been dreaming. Tom, this war isn't going to blight our love forever. When I wrote, I told you that your baby is growing inside me. So please come home safely to me, my darling.*

At that moment, Tom was falling into the sun. And one day not too far hence, a young woman would climb the green hill above Ridgeton with a young boy beside her, guiding his footsteps.

CPSIA information can be obtained at www.ICGtesting.com
Printed in the USA
BVOW02*2358201013

334046BV00001B/1/P